MW01482806

Constable Stephen Grant
of
The North-West Mounted Police

in

The Dead Horse Trail

by
Andrew Ferns

Madeira Park, British Columbia, Canada

For My Family...

The Dead Horse Trail

Originally published by the author in 2025.

Copyright © 2025 Andrew Ferns

ISBN: 9798311275118

Paperback Edition

Cover Design by Angelique Silberman

All rights reserved. No part of the publican may be reproduced, distributed, or transmitted in any form or by any means, including photocopying, recording or other electronic or mechanical methods, without the prior written consent of the publisher, except in the case of brief quotation embodied in critical reviews and certain other non-commercial uses permitted by copyright law.

This book is a work of fiction. Any names, characters, companies, organizations, places, events, locales and incidents are either used in a fictitious manner or are fictional. Resemblance to actual persons, things living or dead, locales, or events are entirely coincidental.

ABOUT THE AUTHOR

Andrew Ferns is a Canadian filmmaker, writer, and producer with a diverse career spanning film, television, and literature. A graduate of Dalhousie University and Mount Royal University, Andrew's work bridges both the creative and production sides of the industry, offering a unique perspective to his storytelling.

His documentary credits include award-winning projects such as *Captain Cook: Obsession and Discovery* and *Darwin's Brave New World*, both of which earned multiple accolades. He also produced the feature film *Painkillers*, which won the AMPIA Award for Best Dramatic Feature Film.

As a writer, Andrew's debut novel, the supernatural thriller *Disappear: Into Shadow* demonstrated his talent for crafting suspenseful, character-driven narratives. He has also created historical content, including the *Monumental Canadians* web series for Valour Canada, which received numerous accolades.

Beyond film and literature, Andrew has produced bespoke visual content for brands like Enbridge and the Calgary Stampede; and, has worked with The Walt Disney Company, NBC Universal, and HBO overseeing Production Health and Safety on major titles like *Big Sky*, *The Fall Guy*, and *The Last of Us*.

In this latest book, Andrew continues to immerse readers in his world of intricate storytelling, where complex characters and high-stakes tension collide. He resides on the Sunshine Coast of British Columbia, Canada, with his wife, where the landscapes and rich history continue to inspire his creative work.

OTHER WORKS BY THE AUTHOR:
Disappear: Into Shadow   ISBN-13 978-1099933721

CONTENTS

CHAPTER		PAGE
I	THE CLIMB	1
II	THE COST OF PASSAGE	7
III	A BROKEN SILENCE	17
IV	THE HOSTAGE	23
V	THE HIDEOUT	28
VI	THE WAIT	33
VII	TINY FRACTURES	38
VIII	THE ESCAPE	43
IX	DOWN SKAGWAY	49
X	A FRAGILE TRUST	56
XI	THE BURDEN OF THE BADGE	62
XII	BETRAYAL IN THE SNOW	70
XIII	AN UNLIKELY MESSENGER	75
XIV	BLOOD IN THE SNOW	81
XV	A TRAITOR ON THE TRAIL	85
XVI	NO MAN'S LAND	91
XVII	THE RACE TO WHITE PASS	96
XVIII	THE HUNTER BECOMES THE HUNTED	101
XIX	A MESSAGE IGNORED	110
XX	AMBUSH!	116
XXI	THE CHASE	122
XXII	THE LOG CABIN	130
XXIII	THE DEFENCE	137
XXIV	THE ATTACK	145
XXV	THE LAST STAND	155
XXVI	THE PRICE	165
XXVII	A NEW ENEMY	171
XXVIII	A NEW POST	179

THE DEAD HORSE TRAIL

1896. THE KLONDIKE. GOLD WAS FOUND!

IN THE RUSH TO REACH THE YUKON, 100,000 PEOPLE MADE THEIR JOURNIES.

ONLY 40,000 EVER REACHED THE GOLD FIELDS.

THE PEACE, AND THE ALASKAN BORDER, WAS HELD BY

THE NORTH-WEST MOUNTED POLICE

OVER

THE DEAD HORSE TRAIL

CHAPTER I

The Climb

Wind. Whiteness. This was a wasteland through which a narrow, winding path cut through snow and ice. As it stretched upwards into the Alaskan peaks of the Coastal Mountains, each step taken up it felt as though it was a climb further into oblivion. The trail was no mere obstacle: it was a gauntlet; a cruel passage that would take every ounce of strength and resolve each Stampeder had and would then demand more. Every inch of progress felt like an eternity to them. And as they climbed, the bitter reality of the trail set in for every foot gained, two were lost.

At the end of this journey lay the promise and ecstasy of gold. Riches beyond belief that were just lying on the ground, waiting to be snatched up by their eager hands. In the end, the lure of twenty-four carats was only a behemoth of a stick. One that would strike them again, and again and again.

For days, each new Stampeder had trudged forward, dragging their sleds and wagons through snowdrifts that reached up to their knees, the weight of their burdens sinking with every step. It was the kind of cold that gnawed at the skin, that slipped through the cracks in their coats and clawed at their bones. It was the kind of cold that made the promise of gold seem a distant, laughable thing.

Horses stumbled behind and ahead, their hooves slipping on the ice. Their breaths were plumes of white in the frigid air. Heavily laden with supplies, these animals, both horse and man alike, strained, their bodies trembling from the unrelenting cold. Some had already fallen dead, frozen in place, and the Stampeders could do little more than keep moving past or walk over the bodies. Among an assortment of abandoned gear, their skeletons and rib bones stick out high and bare from the snow. The trail had claimed them, their bodies scattered along the pass like forgotten relics of a lost cause.

With every forward pull of the sleds away from their starting point in Skagway, the landscape had grown more brutal. The towering pines had thinned, the earth beneath their boots became more treacherous, and the sky overhead closed in like a suffocating weight.

Above them, the mountains were cloaked from view in a deep, swirling and sickly grey. When a break in the storms allowed, the snow-covered peaks came into view, rising sharp and unforgiving, like jagged teeth that cut the sky into sharp pieces. The wind howled across the ridges, a voice that screamed and taunted them as they struggled upward, battling both nature and their own bodies.

"Keep moving!" a man shouted hoarsely, but his voice was swallowed by the wind. His face was a mask of exhaustion, his eyes sunken deep into his skull. His shoulders sagged under the weight of his load, and his clothes clung to his body, soaked with sweat and snow.

The trail's slow, grinding rhythm was a steady, painful crawl. But now, with each new rise in elevation it had become something far worse. The grade was steepening. Each incline felt as though the mountains were pulling themselves back, forcing the climbers to leave the rest of their goods behind just to keep up. The horses strained with every step, their legs shaking, their sides heaving as they pushed against the weight of their poorly loaded packs. But still, they moved, as if the entire group were

THE CLIMB

bound by some unspoken law that there could be no turning back.

One man, a young prospector from Seattle, stumbled and fell to his knees, his legs buckling under the weight of his exhaustion. A few of the others paused, watching him for a moment. There was no time to help, no time to speak. They could only look at him with the same haunted, empty eyes, as if all of them were waiting for the inevitable.

The man tried to rise, his hands slipping on the icy ground. His breath came in sharp, ragged gasps.

"Leave him," someone muttered, their voice flat. It wasn't cruelty, just the hard truth. There were no options here. No mercy. They had been walking through death for days now, the cold gnawing at their bones, the weight of the snow breaking their backs. This was a place where life didn't linger long, and those who couldn't keep up were left behind.

The wind grew colder, colder still, cutting through the layers of their clothing, biting through at the flesh. Each breath felt as though they were inhaling shards of ice. They kept moving, trudging through the snow, the sleds creaking under the weight of their load, the horses' hooves crunching on the frozen ground with each step.

The weather would not give them any respite. Snow squalls blew in without warning, and the trail became a blur of white, the path narrowing, then vanishing altogether in the thick mist. The men shouted over the wind, but their voices were lost. The trail felt like it would swallow them whole. They couldn't see more than a few feet ahead. The bitter cold, the relentless climb: it all seemed to blend into one crushing weight of fatigue.

The snow fell in sheets, falling with such force that it seemed as though the mountains were pouring it down upon them, mocking them with a silent fury. The horses were falling behind now, their strength giving out, their hooves heavy in the deep snow. One by one, the men stopped, kneeling to adjust the harnesses, to prod the horses forward, but the animals were failing. Each one struggled to stand, their eyes glassy, their bodies quivering in the cold.

THE DEAD HORSE TRAIL

At one point, a horse collapsed at the crest of a ridge, its legs buckling beneath it, its side heaving in shallow gasps. A few Stampeders were gathered around it, their faces grim. There was no time to mourn. No time to pause. The load now had to be divided among the men. And so, they did what they had to do, dragging the sleds up the hill despite their already burdened bodies and dwindling energies. The horse was left behind, snow already covering it.

Another body was left behind, this time it was a man who had fallen in the deep snow and could not rise again. His frozen form, covered with a layer of snow, became nothing more than a shadow in the wind. No one said anything. He had simply been too slow, too weak to keep moving. And now, the mountain had claimed him as it had claimed so many before.

By now, the trail was barely discernible. The series of twisted, craggy ridges and narrow paths wound up the sheer face of the pass. It was as though the mountain had been built to break those who dared to scale it. At one point, a man's hand slipped from his sled's rope, and he tumbled backward, sliding down the icy slope. He screamed, and yet another sound was lost to the wind.

Further ahead, amid the thick curtains of blowing snow, two figures emerged from the swirling depths, descending in a clumsy rush. Without only small packs on their backs, as they stumbled around a bend in the trail.

Downhill, a single Stampeder lead his two pack horses up the steep slope. When one of the horses went lame, it faltered, stumbled, then fell to the snow. The Stampeder, yanked suddenly backwards by the reins, cried out in dismay, "Goddammit!"

Shaking off the snow, he rose and tied off his other horse to the fallen one's pack. Inspecting the horse's leg, he could see it had shattered. There was no help he could offer. The poor beast was suffering, neighing and huffing in pain. Drawing out a revolver from his coat, his numb hands fumbled with the action. Drawing the hammer back, his finger wrapped around the trigger. With a pull and jerk, he fired a single shot into its head. The report of the shot was swiftly swallowed up by the storm as the horse lay still and silent.

THE CLIMB

"Son-of-a-bitch! Really!?" the Stampeder yelled as he considered what to do next. As he stared at the body, the pair of descending figures approached him. They were Klondikers: those who had crossed the mountains and seen what there was to see on the other side. Now, they were making their return, or escape, back to the civilized world. Or so they hoped.

One of them asked the Stampeder, "Hey Mister, you still need that?"

"No. Hey, what? My supplies? Yes. Of course I do. Back off, or I'll put one in ya." He snarled and pointed the revolver in their direction, "I got one for each of ya."

"Not your outfit, Mister. We don't want that." The Klondiker replied. His compatriot added, "That horse. The dead one."

"What? No. Not anymore," he replied with surprise.

"Can we have it?"

"Huh? What, for?"

"Whaddya think?" The Klondiker challenged him as the snow began to ease back and clear the air. A lull in the storm, finally. "Can we have it, or not?"

"Hey, you two back off. Now!" The Stampeder yelled and waved his revolver back and forth between the men.

Further down the slope, the next wave of climbers appeared from the clearing fog. The sharp report of a gunshot echoed down across the slope. The lead packhorse jumped in surprise from the shot. The man leading it calmed the horse and continued to climb. Ahead, he now sees a struggle for life and death between Stampeder and Klondiker. The other Klondiker lay dead on the ground, a red stain spreading outwards across his chest.

As the two men wrestled, another gunshot rang out and the Stampeder dropped to the ground, clutching at a wound in his belly. The Klondiker stood over the dying man, revolver in hand and screamed, "What now? Bastard! What now? Hey?"

The lead man in the approaching group answered the question with, "Forwards!"

Exasperated, the Klondiker replied, "No, man. Back! Turn back!"

The clearing in the snowfall retreated as swiftly as it had appeared. The gathered storm's anger returned, engulfing the

5

THE DEAD HORSE TRAIL

snaking long trail of people once more in a renewed blizzard. Looking like a chain of ants, the Stampeders continued their climb ignoring the Klondiker's warning and plea.

CHAPTER II

The Cost of Passage

After what had felt like an eternity, the seemingly endless snow and fog cleared. Out from what had once been an impenetrable pale blur of shifting clouds, a new horizon appeared. The mountain peaks that earlier in the ascent had once loomed like distant, silent gods were no longer hidden. Their jagged faces now stood immediate and menacing above them.

Now, at last, they saw it. The outpost.

The unforgiving climb had offered them no mercy, no rest, just an endless struggle against the elements. And yet here, at the end of this treacherous route, stood a collection of buildings: small and rough-hewn they were barely more than half buried shelters against the ever-present wind and snow. Known as the Log Cabin, the White Pass Outpost was the official border crossing from America into the Dominion of Canada.

The fluttering Union Jack and the Stars and Stripes were the only flashes of colour in this land of white and grey. The sight of the outpost was both a relief and a curse. These Stampeders had made it this far, but at what cost? The men and horses were little more than ghosts themselves, hollow-eyed and barely able to stand. Faces blank from exhaustion, they dragged their loads, sleds and bodies towards this non-existent finish line. It was the first stage of a lethal marathon.

Though the blizzards had passed, the wind remained a scream that cut through the travellers like a blade. Their faces were pale and raw from the wind, their clothes soaked through despite the thick layers of wool and fur. They had come through hell to get here, and this outpost was no more than a stop, a brief, cold respite before the plunge downhill into a greater unknown.

For the Stampeders, there was no joy in arrival. The mountains had stripped them bare. The journey had taken everything they had. The Dead Horse Trail had taken its toll, and those who had survived would carry its weight with them forever.

Nestled against the rocks, the outpost looked out of place in this desolate landscape. An oddity. There was no welcoming warmth to be found in its structures, no safety in the way the buildings were huddled against the mountain's edge. Instead, it felt like a holding pen for those foolish enough to think they could tame the land through a final bastion of order, a structure of government and regulation that sat unyielding against the savage wilderness.

The North-West Mounted Police were stationed here, not to help, but to keep order, to see that the river of men who would try to reach the goldfields, were funnelled through the Pass with a measure of discipline and paid for the privilege in customs duties.

From inside the Log Cabin itself, smoke from the wood stove mixed with pipe tobacco as it curled up to the rafters. The smell of damp wool mixed with the dry, musty scent of wood and stale, unwashed clothing. The wind whistled through the gaps in the wooden walls, rattling them like a child's toy. A collection of uniformed men sat around the cabin, reading, writing, whittling and passing the time between arrivals as best they could. The scarlet red of their uniform serge coats stood in stark colourful contrast to the rough wooden walls.

Inspector D'Arcy Strickland looked through a small window down towards the approaching traffic. "Looks like a new batch have made it," he muttered. "Look at these poor beggars. Not one of them knows what they're stumbling towards."

He finished his mug of coffee and wiped away the residue from his prodigious black moustache. He twitched his nose, then set the battered tin mug down on the wood stove by the window. "Best we go have a look at this lot. On your feet lads."

Without any dissent, the four other men in the cabin stood and begin wrapping themselves up in their buffalo jackets and peaked fur hats. Mittens are pulled on and Winchester Repeater rifles were hoisted up from the racks against walls of the cabin. These Constables were Strickland's law and order on the Pass and it was a peace he meant to keep.

As they stepped out of the relative warmth of the cabin and into the mountain air, he issued his orders, "You two: take up the Maxim and stand ready. You two: on me."

The Constables split up with Strickland and his group setting off downhill towards the rudimentary border. The other two Constables climbed up to a fortified position of sandbags and rough logs. Behind this position was a Maxim machinegun, mounted on an iron tripod. One Constable fetched a box of ammunition, while the other opened the top of the gun.

Setting it down beside the gun, the Constable opened the box and fished out a canvas belt, loaded with bullets and handed it one end to the other man. The gunner fed the belt into the gun and then closed the breech, racked the action and stood ready. The other Constable raised up a pair of binoculars and trained them on Strickland the others as they waited for the new arrivals.

As Strickland watched the weary travellers' approach, his uniform pants were stiff with the cold, but he stood tall, his posture a rigid contrast to the bent figures of the Stampeders.

From the distance, it looked like this handful of people, each struggling, each bearing the same vacant expression were lost in their own private exhaustion. They were all the same shade of weary, all had been swallowed up by winter's hungry maw. The heavy packs were sagging low on their backs, their sleds and horses laden with the very weight of their hopes, and their desperation.

THE DEAD HORSE TRAIL

One man, a tall figure wrapped in a fur-lined coat, stepped ahead of the group, his eyes squinting against the wind. He reached up and adjusted his hat, his face streaked with salt and grime from the days of walking.

He gestured to his companions and his voice, hoarse voice from days of shouting against the wind, said, "We're all happy to be here. Aren't we?"

The others didn't respond. They had long since stopped speaking to each other, each wrapped in their own private thoughts, focused only on putting one foot in front of the other. The weather had long since worn them down, leaving them half-empty, drained, unable to summon the energy for anything beyond survival.

And yet, here at the outpost, the first thing they faced wasn't warmth, or shelter, or food but inspection. Under the watchful and lethal gaze of the Maxim machine gun position, the North-West Mounted Police's faces were unreadable amongst their cover of their fur hats and heavy Buffalo coats.

"You've made it," Strickland said. And, while he meant well by saying this, the words were hollow, spoken more as a formality than a greeting. He looked the travellers over, but there was little in his gaze that suggested sympathy. He'd seen this before. In fact, he had seen it many times, day in and day out. Arms folded behind his back, he knew many of the assembled Stampeders would die in the Yukon, or leave, destitute.

"Rest up," he said gruffly, his voice barely audible over the howling wind. "But I wouldn't linger too long. You'll need to be on your way again soon. The weather will never wait for you."

"How long is it to the Yukon?" one man asked, his voice also rasping and dry.

Strickland did not answer right away. He stepped past the first man, eyeing the group. His movements were methodical, practiced. He looked at the next man: the one who asked the question. His eyes were like shards of ice as he replied, "That depends. The Pass might clear. It might not. Another storm may be coming tonight. Could be a week. Could be longer. Twice, three times as long."

THE COST OF PASSAGE

The man nodded, though it was clear he was too tired to comprehend the response. Another storm would pass over them, as it had before, and as it would again. It was the kind of weather that made everything seem pointless, a constant reminder that nature cared little for human plans. The frozen breath of the waiting men and animals alike mingled in the cold. The horses, shivering and spent waited in this brief recess from action. Their coats were matted with snow. Their eyes dull from fatigue as they waited behind their masters.

"Right, line up!" Strickland barked, his voice cutting through the wind. "Your outfits must be inspected, and all duties paid before you can pass."

The Stampeders hesitated for a moment, barely able to lift their arms, too exhausted to move quickly. They had little left to give, their energy long since drained. Strickland stepped toward the first man who had spoken for the group, and asked, "Purpose of your visit?"

Before the Prospector answered, the other Constables began barking orders, "You lot: to the right!"

And the other shouted, "You lot: over here. To the left! To the left!"

Remaining at the centre, the first man replied to Strickland's question, "Prospecting."

Strickland regarded the man and asked, "Heading for Dawson, I presume"?

"Yessir."

"Hmm," was Strickland's terse reply. "These two, Canadian horses?"

"Yessir," the Prospector answered. "The finest in Skagway. They're healthy, as you can see. Great mounts."

"Five dollars a head on them," Strickland replied.

"What?"

"How's your outfit?" Strickland continued. "Got your ton of goods? Food, clothing, equipment?"

"Most of it," the Prospector replied. "I gotta go back for some stashes I left. That was a helluva weight to lug up that trail. Damn treacherous."

"As we've heard," Strickland condescended. "You'll need all of it to survive. Anything else to declare?"

For a moment, the Prospector paused. He considered the Mountie's lack of response to the climb he had just made. "That: was a helluva climb. Like I said, it was treacherous."

Strickland looked the man over for a moment before replying, "Indeed. Constable, take over from here, please."

Without another glance, Strickland walked away from the scene and walked back towards the Log Cabin.

The Prospector repeated his statement as the Constable stepped forwards to took over the interview, "Helluva trail."

The Constable replied, "I wholly agree."

The Prospector pointed up towards the Machine gun nest, "Is that...?"

"A Maxim Gun?" The Constable confirmed, "It is indeed."

"Well, I'll be," he replied.

"Will you now?"

"Yep, sure will. I saw me a Gatling gun once. That was enough for this lifetime. I sure would have to say. And, seeing one angry? A helluva experience that was. Helluva one. One I don't wish to see again. So, I'll wish you a good day, Officer. I come and I go in peace."

"Constable. I ain't no officer. Weapons?"

"I'm sorry, Constable. I meant no offence. No, thank you, I'm good."

"Pardon?" the Constable asked.

"Don't need any. I'm covered," they replied.

The Constable clarified, "I meant: do you have any?"

"Weapons?" asked the Prospector.

"Yes. Guns, knives?"

"Foul language?" was the not mildly sarcastic reply.

"That as well: certainly."

"Then: yes. Of course," the Prospector offered in response.

"To which part?"

"Of what?" asked the Prospector.

"To which part?"

"Whaddaya mean?"

12

THE COST OF PASSAGE

The Constable set his shoulders back and leant forward. He then asked, pointedly, "Do. You. Have. Weapons? Guns? Knives? Foul language?"

Without hesitation they replied, "Hell yeah. Correct."

The Constable stared straight at him after the response, incredulous. During the awkward pause between statements, the Prospector then added, "All of them, goddammit."

The Constable looked around and spat out a simple, "Shit."

"I know, tell me about it," came the simple reply.

"Seriously?"

"My hand to God. On my mother's grave," was the final reply that did not elaborate further.

Reclaiming any sense of decorum, the Constable pivoted in his inquiry, "Any dynamite? Explosives? Bear traps?"

"No, no. No?" the Prospector replied.

"Fine," the Constable replied. "You got five hundred in cash?"

"Yeah."

"Customs duty for you to cross is then, ah, thirty-seven fifty," the Constable stated.

"Thirty-seven?" the Prospector asked. "Dollars?"

"Yes."

Next came the inevitable questions, "For what? Carrying all this up here?"

"Correct. And you if don't like it: you can carry it all back downhill. Likely by yourself. These horses of yours: three to one odds that..." the Constable paused as he checked the horse's condition, running his hands over its rib cage and flanks. "This one's alright."

Shifting his inspection to the other horse, he replicated his movements with a practised detachment. "This one? She'll likely die on the descent. So, yeah: it costs you thirty-seven fifty. In dollars. To cross, today, with what you have on you."

"Seems mighty predatory, that duty," the Prospector rebutted.

"You're welcome to turn around and head back," the Constable countered. "Now, it's fifty."

"Like I said: Predatory," the Prospector replied. "Take your damn money. Here."

"Fifty, I said."

13

THE DEAD HORSE TRAIL

"Fifty? For what?" was the pointless question asked. "Here's forty. Keep the change."

"And another ten..."

"Damn it, fine then. Here's the ten. What's that for?" asked the Prospector.

"This," replied the Constable as he tucked the ten dollars into the folds of his Buffalo Coat.

"You're kidding me!"

"Move along, Argonaut," said the Constable. "Move along."

"I should've taken the Chilkoot Trail instead."

"And maybe you just should've stayed home," the Mountie shot back.

The other, younger Constable called out to his compatriot, "Hey Dorsey? Can you help me out with this?"

He was looking over another man's horse. The grey mare stood unsteadily, her legs trembling beneath her, her breath shallow. Constable Dorsey stepped forward and ran his hands over her flank, his fingers pressing against her ribs. The animal flinched and whinnied, but she had no strength left to protest.

"Sick," Dorsey's voice was flat and emotionless. "You can't carry her through to the Yukon," he said to the Stampeder. He turned to the other Constable and added, "You know the rules."

The Stampeder froze. There was a beat of silence. The man's face was hollow with exhaustion. He was young, his hair dark and matted with sweat and snow. His hands, already stiff from the cold, trembled as he reached out to the horse's neck.

"She's not sick," he said quietly, his voice shaking as if he didn't quite believe the words himself.

Dorsey, didn't answer the man, but said to the other Constable, "I'll leave you to it, Thompson." He returned to the other queue of Stampeders and barked, "Next!"

"She just needs a rest. A day?" the Stampeder pleaded.

"She's not fit for the journey," Constable Thompson replied. "You'll have to leave her here. There's no room for dead weight."

The young Stampeder's mouth opened, but the words never came. There was nothing he could say. Thompson turned to the nearest mount, his rifle at the ready. With one clean shot, the mare's legs buckled beneath her. The sound of it echoed across

THE COST OF PASSAGE

the snow-covered landscape, final and cold, like the very mountains themselves had just claimed another soul.

The man stood silent, his face a mask of stunned disbelief. Some of the others turned away. There was nothing to be done.

"That's one less to feed," Constable Dorsey observed without a trace of sympathy.

The rest of the horses were inspected, each one assessed for its fitness and its strength to carry on. The sick ones, the weak ones, the ones that could no longer stand, each was put down in the same cold, indifferent manner. The cost of the journey was not just measured in food or supplies. It was paid in blood, in the death of animals who had borne the brunt of the travel through the mountains, their strength finally exhausted.

Next, the sleds were inspected, their contents checked one by one. Packs of flour, bacon, beans, and the occasional bag of dried fish were weighed and catalogued. For each item, the Constables made a note, and the Stampeders were asked to pay the customs duty: a fee to enter the Klondike. A fee to live. There were grumbled protests from a few of the men, their voices raw with fatigue, but it was all routine, all part of the price they had to pay. There was no room for negotiation here - just survival.

Each item of the load, the tools, the picks, the shovels, and the tents, were scrutinized, and the customs fees piled up with each new piece. Those who couldn't pay were ordered to turn back and return to Skagway, their hopes and gilded dreams crushed. A few broke down, their voices cracking with frustration and sorrow. What had they endured the mountains for? Just to be taxed for the right to continue?

"I paid my duties in Skagway!" one man shouted, shaking his fist at Constable Dorsey.

The Mountie's response was swift, cold, and unfeeling. "We don't collect duties in down in Skag. You pay them here. Or, turn yourself around take it up with the ones who robbed you."

The hours stretched on. As the Stampeders' loads were dismantled and reassessed, the men and women who had endured the worst of the trail stood, silent and defeated, watching as the money they had scraped together was taken from them, one heavy coin at a time.

THE DEAD HORSE TRAIL

When the inspections were over and the last of the unfit horses had been shot, the Constables turned and nodded to the final member of the group, "You're free to pass."

But there was no joy. There was no triumph. The Stampeders were too far gone for that. The weight of the journey, of the animals they had lost, of the goods and money they had surrendered - it all hung on their shoulders like a burden they could never shake. Some of the men turned away immediately after their release and continued their journeys, unwilling to look at their companions, unwilling to meet the cold gaze of the Constables. Others simply slumped to the ground, too tired to speak, as though the simple act of standing had become too much.

The lands beyond the outpost now were open to them. The Dominion of Canada lay ahead, but the that next step of the journey was a road which promised no more kindness than the one they had just survived. The Yukon waited for them, just beyond this new horizon. And the Stampeders, those who had made it this far, now knew that the next test was only just beginning.

CHAPTER III

A Broken Silence

Constable Stephen Grant stood at the edge of the river, his tall black riding boots crunching softly on the thin crust of snow that coated the frozen ground. His breath misted in the air, vanishing almost instantly as the wind picked up, carrying the sharp bite of winter from the northeast. It was a cruel wind, one that cut through every layer of wool, fur, and leather, and left nothing but cold in its wake. The mountains loomed to the west. Their jagged peaks barely visible through a heavy shroud of low-hanging clouds. The Yukon had a way of swallowing the world whole, of making even the boldest men feel small.

    Grant tugged his thick Buffalo coat tighter around his frame, the weight of it was heavy against the freezing air. Its broad shawl collar was wrapped around his face, his breath freezing as it fell on the fur. The cuffs were cinched tight against the wind, but it wasn't enough to keep the cold from seeping in. His mittens were worn and stiff from the harsh conditions of constant travel, the tips of his fingers almost numb despite the protection. As he adjusted his peaked fur cap we see his face. A few weeks' worth of growth lined his square jaw. He preferred to stay clean shaven, but the cold and this extended patrol had made it impossible to keep up. At least the beard kept some of his face less chapped and raw from the wind. His green eyes squinted through the day's gloom. The days were getting shorter, the sun barely rising above the horizon before sinking again, and the cold had begun to feel like an old companion, its presence gnawing at the edge of every thought.

He stood there for a moment, staring at the dark river stretching out before him. The water moved sluggishly, as if reluctant to flow, frozen in places where the ice had taken hold. Along its banks, the gnarled pine trees rustled in slow unison. The virtual silence was absolute, save for the faint sound of his boots crunching in the snow. In the distance, a raven cawed, the three calls sharp and alone, before they disappeared into the thin mists. The Yukon wilderness was vast, indifferent to the men who tried to make a life within it.

Behind him a low whinny brought him back to the present. He turned to look at his mount, Hannah, a bright chestnut mare just a shade over fourteen hands tall. He had originally arrived in the Yukon with a much taller Ontario born stallion, but the harsh conditions soon had taken their toll. Hannah was a native pony, brought up from Alberta. These smaller, tougher breeds were better suited to the long, hard patrols without proper forage and shelter.

Patting her neck Grant whispered, "There, there. Who's my good girl?"

He wanted to disturb the silence as little as possible. He had grown used to it. With a smooth, practised motion he swung himself up into the California saddle. Slipping his boots into the stirrups he heard the jangle of his spurs. Hanging from the pommel, he adjusted the strap of his 1876 Winchester repeater carbine to keep it hanging flush against her shoulder. Taking the reins, he swung Hannah around and pushed back into the forest.

Grant was a member of the Tagish Post of the North-West Mounted police. He had been out on patrol from the Post, otherwise known as Fort Sifton, for weeks now. His job was to maintain some semblance of order in this frozen land. Fuelled by the constant rumours of more gold in Dawson City, reports of illegal mining, whiskey smuggling, and other criminal activities were on the rise. Every day, new faces appeared in the region. These miners, traders and drifters were looking for their fortune. Each of them was willing to bend or break the law to get it.

There was no easy way to enforce order in a place like this, but Grant tried, even if it meant standing alone in the freezing cold, waiting for a glimpse of something, anything, that would tell him where his duty lay next. The Yukon was a land that tested men, body and spirit, and Grant had long since stopped questioning why he had chosen this life. Maybe it was a sense of duty, maybe it was the cold lure of redemption, but either way, here he was, an officer of the law in the middle of nowhere, waiting for the next report to come in.

Reaching into the folds of his coat, he removed a brass pocket watch. Flipping open its lid, he peered at the face. Despite being kept close against his body, the movement's mechanism was slow from the cold. It read nearly midday. Grant closed the watch and returned it to the relative warmth of his coat. For another moment, he looked around, allowing the landscape to fill him up. The mountains stood as they always were: ancient, eternal, stoic. The boughs of the surrounding trees were bent under the weight of snow. There was no sign of life, no smoke from a fire, no movement. He was alone in the wilderness. It always felt good.

After a few miles of steady riding, he approached a fork in the forest trail. Grant turned Hannah to the take the lefthand trail. His breath swirled out in front of him as something broke the silence.

It wasn't the whisper of the wind or the call of a bird. It was the unmistakable crack of a rifle being fired, followed by the sharp snap of a bullet that passed near his face.

Grant's heart stuttered in his chest. The shot had come from further up the righthand trail. His instincts kicked in immediately, as he reached for the rifle slung on his pommel. He swung it up with practice ease to his hand, then spin cocked the lever action to rack a round into the carbine's chamber. The snow beneath Hannah crunched loudly under her hooves as his mount turned about to face the unknown enemy. His pulse quickened as he moved, eyes darting toward the sound.

A second shot rang out, this time closer, and the bullet snatched at the upper left shoulder of his coat. Grant barely had time to react before the third shot rang out. That shot caught Hannah flush in the forehead and the horse tumbled hard. The world turned upside down as Grant was thrown heavily to the ground. Staring up at the overcast sky, it took the Constable a few moments to collect himself from the hard fall and sudden stop.

As his senses and breath returned, he heard the rustling of movement in the trees ahead. Someone was out there, someone who didn't want to be seen. The wind carried the sound of movement, but the trees themselves were silent, like sentinels watching over this dark, secret battle.

Grant rolled over. He couldn't see anyone yet and couldn't find his rifle. He crawled through the heavy snow and off the trail. Slipping behind a large boulder that jutted out from a snowbank, he listened. He knew this terrain, the way the trees grew and the way the wind twisted through the mountain passes. His mind was already racing through scenarios, calculating the distance, the angle, the possible hiding spots. He had to be careful. One mistake here could cost him everything.

His mind raced, calculating, assessing. There had been rumours of trouble in the area: some whiskey smugglers and illegal mining. But nothing like this. Nothing organized and deadly. Another shot cracked through the air. Grant didn't have time to think. His eyes scanned the surroundings. There, half-hidden in the trees, he saw a group of men in dark clothing. They were moving swiftly from tree to tree, advancing toward him. Their faces were obscured by hoods and scarves, but he knew the type. Outlaws. A gang. The kind of men who had no use for the law.

His pulse quickened, but his training kept him steady. He'd been in worse situations, though never one quite like this. No backup, no time for a plan. His only option was to fight.

But then, as he took a breath to steady himself, he heard another rustle in the trees: behind him. A voice, low, gravelly, and cold cut through the silence, "Don't move, Constable."

Grant's heart lurched. The tone was unmistakable: it was the voice of someone who had no intention of negotiating. He cursed under his breath, silently berating himself for not hearing the first sign of danger sooner. He had become complacent and hadn't expected anyone to be out this far, not in this weather.

Slowly, he moved his hand toward the holster at his right side. He popped the flap to reveal the Adams revolver's grip. Before he could pull it free, a shadow moved out from the trees to his left and revealed itself, mere feet from his hiding spot.

Tall and wiry, the man's features were obscured by a thick scarf and a heavy fur coat, but Grant saw enough to know that this man was a threat. A Henry Repeater was squarely aimed at his chest. The hands did not shake, and the man's eyes were cold, ice-blue, sharp and calculating.

"You're far from your post, Constable," the man said, his voice carrying an edge of amusement. "You out here chasing smugglers? Or are you looking for us?"

Grant didn't answer. His hand was still on the grip of his sidearm, but it was clear that any move he made now would end with a bang and a bullet passing through him.

The man stepped closer, the crunch of his boots in the snow loud against the stillness. He was close enough now that Grant could see that his coat was dark and well-made, his boots were lined with thick fur to keep the cold out. A bandolier of cartridges ran across his chest, and his belt held a pair of revolvers, their dull metal gleamed cold in the daylight.

"I'll tell you what, Constable," the man said with a sly grin, "If you're smart and listen, you may live to see another morning."

Before Grant could respond, more footsteps crunched in the snow as the group of men he had been focussed on arrived. Four of them: all armed and all carried themselves with the same sense of controlled violence. Their rifles all took careful, steady aim on him.

He was surrounded.

Grant's thoughts raced, but his body stayed still. He couldn't make a run for it; he would never make it through the snowdrifts without catching multiple bullets. Even if he could try and fight, the odds were stacked against him.

The first man stepped forward again, this time putting a gloved hand on Grant's shoulder. The hard point of their rifle's muzzle now pressed against his coat to meet his spine.

"Show me your hands."

Grant released his grip on the revolver and raised his hands over his head. Surrender. The inevitability of it felt like a mule kick to the gut.

The man likely smiled behind his scarf when he said, "A wise choice."

"What do you want?" Grant asked, his voice low but firm.

"You're coming with us," the man said. "It's a long road ahead, Constable. But you'll get us what we want."

CHAPTER IV

The Hostage

The wind howled across the river as Grant stumbled along the trail, his hands bound tightly in front of him. The ropes bit into his wrists as his mind worked through his predicament. The bonds were pointless, he thought. In this landscape, without a horse, where would he go? Had he chosen to run, he would never get far or move quick enough to get away.

The cold was a constant presence, sinking deep into his bones despite the thick Buffalo coat he wore. His fur-lined mittens, once pristine despite use, had long since turned caked, muddy and ruined. His sturdy riding boots were now wreathed with ice and snow and had long since stopped being waterproof. He struggled to keep up with the gang across this treacherous terrain. His breath came in ragged bursts, turning to mist in the frigid air.

The sky overhead remained its endless expanse of grey. The heavy clouds that hung low over the mountains trapped the cold between them and the earth. A steady, biting wind made everything feel sharp, sharper than the freezing touch of the snow, sharper than the ache in his muscles, sharper than the weight of the shame of his surrender. That weight felt like a cross cutting into his back as he dragged it towards his eventual place of execution.

His five captors were around him, moving with swift, purposeful strides. They were well-prepared: furs lined their hoods and coats, they wore fine thick mittens and gloves, and all were expert in their use of snowshoes. They cut through the snow with an ease that Grant grew more envious of by the minute. Their faces were obscured by scarves and the frosty air. He had been captured by a gang of criminals, there was no doubt about it.

Their leader kept to the front, his tall, wiry frame a silhouette against the ashen landscape. He had been the first one to speak when Grant had been taken. He was dressed in a heavy, dark coat of fur and wool. His thick leather boots laced high and tight were strapped to those wonderful wood and woven snowshoes. He strode with confidence through the snow, as if he'd known these paths for years. He had a calm authority about him. For a man who'd just ambushed a lawman in the wilderness, he was too composed. These were no first timers.

Were they Trappers, Grant wondered, *or Smugglers?* They exuded the manner of cold and detached confidence that only came from years of living on the edge of the land and the law. Or, perhaps beyond it altogether. Every now and then, the leader would glance back at Grant, but only long enough to ensure that the Constable was still in tow. His expression was unreadable, his ice-blue eyes scanning the horizon with military precision.

"You're lucky," the leader said finally, his voice cutting through the wind. He didn't look back as he spoke, his gaze fixed on the trail ahead. "I was going to kill you outright when we first saw you. But the thing is, we've got bigger plans, and you? You could prove useful."

"Useful?" Grant shot back, his words tinged with bitterness. "You think you'll get away with this?"

The leader drew the scarf down from his face, and now did truly smile. It was a thin, spiteful thing. "The law's a long way from here, Constable. And if you're smart, you'll start thinking about how you can help us get what we need."

Grant didn't respond. He'd learned the futility of talking to men like this. Men who thought they controlled the world because they'd survived long enough, taking whatever they wanted without punishment. He didn't need to explain himself. He just needed to survive.

"Good, best you stay quiet. You've got a good head on your shoulders. After all, you had the good sense to surrender. A lawman who knows how to survive. There's a rarity."

As they trudged onward, the gang fell into a loose formation, murmuring amongst themselves. Grant couldn't help but notice the way some of them looked at him, half-curious, half-suspicious. The gang was tight, but there was a tension in the air, a crackling of uncertainty that Grant couldn't place, but he could taste in the cold.

The landscape around them was unforgiving. Jagged peaks rose to their west, their tops lost in the snow and fog, like the teeth of some ancient beast rising from the earth. The trail they followed now wound away from the river, around frozen lakes and through thick stands of pine, the trees bent under the weight of the heavy snow. Every step felt like an eternity, and the constant wind made it impossible to find any warmth.

As they approached a narrow pass between two towering snow caked cliffs, the leader paused. "We'll camp here for the night," he called over his shoulder, his voice barely audible against the wind.

Grant watched and listened as one of the other men approached and asked, "McCade, you sure? A little further and we've got shelter."

McCade replied, "It's not safe to push further in the dark. Make a fire."

Grant's breath clouded in the air, a steady rhythm in the silence. He forced himself to kneel, his legs aching as he settled into the snow. He watched as the gang scattered quickly, setting up camp with an efficiency that spoke of practice. The campfire, built inside a shallow depression in the snow, flickered bright against the wind. The gang were quiet now, speaking in low tones, no one meeting each other's eyes for too long. As the gloom overtook them, the fire's light cast long, trembling shadows across the snow.

Seated in the snow with his back against a rock, Grant stared out at the fire, watching as it sputtered in the wind. His breath was ragged in his chest. The rope around his wrists chafed but he didn't dare struggle, it wouldn't help. Not yet. He would wait for the right moment. The Constable's mind was sharp, and he kept his gaze fixed on the leader's movements. He was studying the man as he pulled a bundle from his pack and sat down with a small notebook. *McCade, so, you're a man of letters*, Grant told himself.

Grant's thoughts were interrupted by a quiet voice, "You look cold."

He turned to see one of the gang members, standing just a few feet away. They wore a fur-lined parka that swallowed their frame, the hood pulled up and a scarf over their face to shield them from the wind. There was something in their eyes that hinted at a quieter storm beneath the surface.

"Nothing sneaks past you," Grant replied. His voice was hoarse, but he didn't care to socialize. "It'll be our little secret."

They didn't reply, but took a step closer, their boots crunching softly on the snow. Their hands, gloved in fur, shifted at their side then drew a long-handled knife from its scabbard. The gleam of its blade caught the fire's glow for a moment.

"You're not much use to us like this," they muttered, the voice low and gruff. "I'm giving you a little more freedom." They cut the ropes around Grant's wrists. "We aren't the only thing holding you captive. The Yukon does that enough."

For a moment, Grant met their gaze, then nodded slowly. His fingers ached as the blood returned to them from the loosened rope. He could feel the pain spread across his hands, the cold settling deeper in his joints, but he didn't make a sound. Instead, he forced himself to relax, his mind focused on an escape that was still distant, still faint, but perhaps just within reach.

"You should have patrolled somewhere else," they said. Looking at him with something that bordered on sympathy. Or was it guilt? "This life doesn't end well for people like you. For people like us."

There was something different in the voice. It was softer. Grant didn't react when his cold numbed brain figured it out. "This is exactly how I like to spend my time," he said, his voice low. "I'm here because I have a job to do. And you?" He paused, "You here by choice?"

Their gaze flickered for a moment, as if considering his words. Then they looked away, scanning the camp. "Absolutely," they said.

"What's a woman doing with this bunch of criminals?" Grant asked. "You're not like them."

Stepping to closer to Grant, they pulled down their scarf to reveal their face. It was hard, worn by the sun, wind and unspoken hurts. Her eyes hardened to a pointed edge as she said, "The hell I ain't. You don't know anything about me, Copper."

"I know enough," Grant replied. "If you were like them, you'd have left me tied up to freeze."

She didn't respond. Instead, she just kept her eyes forward, her mouth set in a tight line. Grant noticed the slight tremor in her hands before she turned away.

"Thank you," he called after her.

Grant watched her walk past the fire and the other gang members. Her figure was swallowed by the darkness and the snow. The fire crackled nearby, but it did little to warm him. Perhaps he had found some hope for the trail ahead. He just had to hold on to it and survive this night.

CHAPTER V

The Hideout

The following morning, the camp was broken by first light. The overcast sky and the lack of any real sun kept the world frozen in an eternal twilight's murk. The clouds hung dull, heavy and grey above them, threatening more snow to crush the earth beneath it. The temperature had dropped even further overnight, and Grant could feel the frost biting at his skin, creeping through his layers of wool and fur. He legs felt heavy and his thoughts were thick, jumbled.

The gang moved out, leaving behind only the faded tracks of their boots in the snow. Grant felt the cold had now become a distinct part of him and had settled into his bones, never to leave. His breath came out in a series of sharp bursts as he trudged along behind the others.

McCade, leading the group, didn't pause for a moment. His eyes scanned the horizon. He didn't speak much, and the others didn't need words to follow him. They moved like shadows, knowing their roles.

The landscape around them grew even more unforgiving. The wind picked up, howling between the ridges and making the snow

THE DEAD HORSE TRAIL

swirl around them, cutting at Grant's exposed face. The path grew steeper and more treacherous. Grant had not been up through this remote area before. Each step felt heavier than the last, his boots sinking into the snow, the biting wind howling around them. He stumbled and fell to the snow, at the edge of exhaustion and exposure.

"We're not stopping," McCade growled. "Get him up. We're close now."

And they did. After the group crested one final ridge, Grant saw a distant, isolated homestead below. In a clearing amongst the pines was a large cabin, a barn, and a series of small snow shrouded outbuildings. Smoke wafted up from the cabin's chimney. The prospect of warmth at first gave him a flash of renewed energy, but soon Grant's heart sank. He realized the gang had made it to their hideout and he had no plan to stop whatever they were up to.

Grant kept his eyes on the ground, trying not to trip on the uneven trail down into the valley, but it was hard to focus on anything other than the constant ache in his muscles and the gnawing cold in his chest. Grant's mind was still working, trying to calculate his next move, but the more he thought about it, the clearer it became that escape was unlikely. The gang was too well-armed, too well-organized and there was nowhere to run. He'd been on the move for days now, his feet numb and his body growing weaker with every step. Even if he managed to break free, there was no guarantee he'd make it far enough to alert his fellow Constables of the NWMP. Not in this weather. Not in these conditions.

Looking up, the homestead was now just ahead of them. Grant decided the only chance he had now was patience.

As the wind whistled through the trees, its icy claws scratched at the wood walls of the cabin. Constable Grant, no longer bound, but still very much a prisoner was shoved roughly through the door. He staggered but managed to keep his balance, his eyes scanning the small, dimly lit cabin. In the corner, a fire crackled, dry and very much alive in a broad iron stove, casting flickering shadows through its grate. A young man was stoking the fire in the stove and looked startled at the new arrival.

THE HIDEOUT

"Who the hell is that?" he asked, but no one answered. The gang sprawled about the room, pulling off their cold, wet layers. The wall of heat inside hit Grant's chapped face with both pain and relief. The warmth was immediate but foreign.

The smell of wet wood and stale air filled his nostrils, mixed with the acrid scent of tobacco smoke. There were no windows, only a single door, which now shut behind him with a thud. McCade, stepped to the stove, his broad shoulders and tall silhouette looming sharp against the warm glow. His face, weathered by years of crime and cold, was a mask of indifferent cruelty.

"Well, well, Constable," McCade's voice cut through the silence, rough as gravel. "You made it. I was thinking you might just freeze to death out there. Have a seat, take a load off."

Grant clenched his teeth and sunk to the floor. His body ached but his mind was stronger than they thought. He had to think. He had to make a plan; but, first he had to warm up. He had to rest. He had to... had to... Blackness took him as he slumped to one side and slept.

It had been a dreamless sleep. A black void, an oblivion. When his eyes opened, Grant was warm, but it was a world of pain that welcomed his return to consciousness. Everything hurt. He rolled over and sat up when a coughing fit racked his chest. He spat out mucus, dirt and anger.

"Good morning," McCade voice rang out. "Welcome back to the land of the living." He was seated at a table nearby. As Grant looked over, he saw the man's eyes gleamed with dark amusement.

"What's the plan?" Grant croaked.

"We're here, and we're going to stay put."

Two others sat with him at the rough-hewn table, playing cards. They looked at him like vultures waiting for a feast. "We've got time to kill," he continued. "Just don't try anything foolish, or we'll have you tied up. Again."

"I got rope if you need it," the new member of the gang offered up. He was much younger than the others and seemed eager to please. Grant presumed he must have been left behind to mind the hideout.

"We don't need it," McCade snapped. "Do we Constable?" Grant shook his head.

"I didn't think so. See? Nothing to worry about Finley. Get the man some water though."

The fire crackled again, and Grant took a steadying breath. His thoughts turned inward. There was a part of him, some small flicker of hope, that still believed the law could save the territory, that it could hold the chaos, like this, at bay. Every day he spent in this lawless place had chipped away at that belief. This land, this godforsaken wilderness, had a way of changing men. Even the most steadfast could lose themselves in the endless white. He had seen it before, with the hardened criminals and desperate miners, but now he was part of the equation. Was there a way out of this?

The young man offered Grant a battered mug. Grant gratefully took the mug and slurped down the freezing cold liquid in greedy slurps. It burned as it went down it was so cold. It brought a new racking series of coughs. When Grant collected himself, he returned the mug and said, "Thanks."

His gaze flicked towards the door. The wind howled outside, but somewhere beyond the door lay his escape, his chance to restore order.

"You might think you can escape," McCade continued, taking a long swig from a half-empty whiskey bottle. "But where would you go? We've got plans. Like it or not, you're a part of them now."

Grant's eyes narrowed, focusing on the subtle movements of the men. His instincts as a lawman kicked in. McCade had a larger agenda. There was something deeper here, something more dangerous. Looking around the cabin, he did not see the woman who had cut his bonds the night before.

The door creaked open, and she entered along with a harsh gust to remind everyone how bad it was outside. Slamming the door shut, she stomped the snow from her boots. Pulling down the hood of her coat, she unwrapped her scarf. Her face was flushed from the cold. She moved with purpose towards the stove, her steps firm.

THE HIDEOUT

"Everything's fine outside," she said, her voice cool and steady. "I've checked the horses. No signs of trouble."

McCade gave a half-hearted wave in reply, barely glancing up at her from his cards. "Good. Keep your eyes open."

One of the other men in the card game joked, "Why don't you make yourself useful and make the Copper some breakfast?"

A few of the others gang members guffawed at the jibe. The woman's eyes hardened, and her hand gripped the knife hilt at her waist. It was subtle, almost imperceptible, but Grant caught it.

McCade said, "That's not the worst idea. Get the Constable some food why don't you?"

"And get me a steak while yer at it!" the other man added. More laughter, but it was cut short as McCade threw a short jab catching the man square across the jaw. The blow knocked the man off his chair and to the floor.

Looking up, blood on his lip, he exclaimed, "Damn it! What the hell, Jerry?"

"Watch your mouth, Harries. Lillian ain't your cook; or, yours to order around. Got it?"

"I got it, I got it." Harries replied as he gathered himself up from the floor.

"While you're up you can get all of us some food. The Constable included. There's a good man."

Harries, eyes filled with rage, was about to protest, but could not compete with the menacing glare of McCade. He shuffled over to the stove without further protest.

"Good man," McCade repeated. "There's a free chair now, Constable. Join me."

CHAPTER VI

The Wait

Lillian, the quiet woman with sharp eyes, leaned against the corner near the stove. Her cigarette glowed faintly in the cabin's gloom. She hadn't said much in the past hours since the meagre food had been served. Her presence lingered in Grant's mind. She wasn't like the others. Grant had been right in that presumption. There was something about her that made him wonder if she was running from something deeper than the law. He had seen it before, a yearning for redemption that glowed in the eyes of those who didn't know how to live without guilt.

Grant's attention remained fixed on her. Lillian certainly wasn't a fool. She wasn't entirely part of McCade's ruthless gang either, not in the same way the others. Was she a potential ally? Or was she just another pawn, like him, in McCade's game, each trying to survive in this frozen wilderness?

As Lillian moved past the card table towards the set of crude bunk beds built against the cabin's far wall, she threw a quick glance at Grant. It wasn't much, just a flicker in her eyes that suggested to Grant that she wasn't entirely loyal to McCade's cause. If anyone here could help him, he felt it would be her.

However, she was not to be underestimated. Grant watched as she swung herself up onto an upper bunk with a graceful ease.

The cold outside was nothing compared to the isolation he felt inside the suffocating cabin. It wasn't just the physical separation from these men, from civilization, it was a moral isolation. The line between right and wrong was becoming increasingly blurred. His badge, the symbol of the North-West Mounted Police felt like a hollow symbol in this wilderness. He feared that his survival could mean breaking the very laws he was sworn to uphold.

Grant's thoughts swirled, *Morality in a lawless land*. The principles he had sworn to uphold felt so far away now. Here, in this stark wilderness it was the survival of the fittest. And everyone, even the most hardened criminals, were running from something. Some ran from the law; some ran from their past. And some were just running. He suspected Lillian was doing all three.

Grant's gaze swept the room. His mind worked quickly, parsing the threat of each person in turn. He had to keep his head. There was no way out unless he could manipulate the situation and find a way to break the gang's cohesion. Grant was torn. He had always believed in redemption, that even the worst of men could turn around, given the right push. But was it too late for these criminals? For himself? If he was going to escape, if he was going to make it out of this situation alive, he would need to rely on someone like Lillian. Someone who could see the grey areas of life in this frozen wilderness. But there was no guarantee she'd help him. And even if she did, the price might be too high.

At the far side of the cabin, Lillian was absently drumming her fingers against the edge of her bunk, lost in thought. Grant could feel the tension thickening in the air. The gang was nervous. They were too quiet, too watchful. And the way McCade's eyes kept flicking back toward the door told him everything he needed to know. They were waiting for something, or someone. Then it hit him. The gang were expecting someone to meet them there.

"Tomorrow," McCade's voice, low and even, broke through his thoughts. "We'll head out."

"Once the rest of your crew shows up?" Grant asked.

"How very perceptive. That's right, Grant. When the others arrive."

THE WAIT

"How many more?"

"Well, that would be telling. Wouldn't it?" McCade replied. The others at the table chuckled as they looked at their cards. "We are legion."

"You're a horde of demons then?"

McCade leaned back slightly in his chair, eyes narrowed, measuring Grant. "A man who knows his scripture. No, even though this lot may think they are the most unholy of the unholy, we're all just men."

"Except for her?" Grant observed.

"Oh no, don't get it twisted. She's a man too. Just as deadly as any of us. Raise you ten."

A collective groan echoed around the table. The remaining men folded their hands. McCade chuckled, tossed his cards onto the table and collected the small pile of nuggets at its centre. "Are you sure you won't play, Grant? Helps pass the time."

"I was never one for cards. I don't remember the rules."

"For a lawman, that's saying something," McCade chuckled, the sound low and harsh.

"As a lawman it would be remiss of me not to say: when the Mounted Police find out what's happened to me, they won't stop until they hunt you all down."

"I'm sure they'll come looking. But you forget, Constable, this place is vast. We know how to disappear. And when we do, you'll be the last person they'll ever hear from." There was a venomous edge to McCade's tone that made Grant's stomach tighten. The man was dangerous, ruthless and smart. "For now, you're still breathing. That's something."

The words settled in the room like a thick fog. The fire crackled and popped in the corner, but its warmth now felt distant. Grant swallowed; his throat was dry. He refused to give McCade the satisfaction of seeing him flinch or show any weakness. "Something I hope to continue doing. Perhaps I will take you up on that drink."

McCade laughed, "That's more like it! Lillian, get the man a mug."

"I'm laying down. The Copper's got legs."

"Fair enough," McCade replied. "Help yourself Grant."

As Grant rose and walked to the stove. Keeping his silence, Grant observed the group. In this cabin, silence was his weapon, and he needed every advantage he could get.

Harries, the man McCade had punched and who had begrudgingly made food, was passed out snoring near the warmth of the cast iron stove. Grant retrieved a mug and turned back to the table.

At the back of the cabin he saw Milton, who had mostly kept to himself since they arrived, was asleep on a lower bunk with his back to the rest of the cabin.

"You're wasting good liquor on that Copper," Lillian observed.

"I'll be the judge of that," McCade snorted.

Grant noticed Lillian turned to stare at McCade's after he spoke. The look in her eyes was not a friendly one. She turned away and stared back at the cabin roof, seeming as though she wanted to be anywhere else entirely.

Sitting back down at the table, Grant slid the mug towards McCade. As a healthy measure of whiskey was poured into it, Grant surveyed the others at table. There was Riggs, a burly man with a jagged scar crossing his forehead. He dealt the cards with a faraway look in his eyes. Beside him was Finley, the youngest member of the gang. His hands were fidgeting with the corner of his shirt, and he looked over his shoulder every few seconds. There was something in the way he swallowed nervously whenever McCade looked in his direction that made Grant suspicious. Finley wasn't just filled with palpable nervous energy, he was afraid. And when men were afraid, they did desperate things.

Taking a swig from his mug, the cheap and terrible alcohol bit into the back of his throat. Grant gasped, saying, "There's a flavour for you."

The other men around the table broke into laughter.

McCade agreed, "You're not wrong, but it'll cure what ails you."

The hours had dragged on and while the card games ended McCade's drinking continued. Riggs and Finley had settled down to sleep on the remaining empty bunks, preparing for another journey ahead. Grant's mind remained focused as he nursed the whiskey in his mug. He couldn't afford to let his guard down. Trying to formulate a plan, some way to escape seemed impossible.

Despite his continued drinking, McCade seemed no more lethargic or unaware than earlier. The man who had everything and offered nothing all at once. The charismatic leader's voice was velvet and sharp as a knife and he had the actions to match. He was sitting near the stove now, staring into its fire. His hands were steepled before him. He appeared to Grant like a man who was plotting something new. He had a way of looking through people, as though he could peel back their skins and see their thoughts. It was a dangerous skill. Grant knew that McCade was contemplating him, studying him, just as he in turn studied the gang.

"I'm going to turn in," Grant said as he stood up from the table. "Do I need to be tied up?"

McCade shook his head, "No need, I ain't going to sleep. You enjoy your rest, Grant."

His back to McCade, Grant caught Lillian's eye as he passed her bunk. There was something unreadable in her expression, something conflicted. Grant couldn't be sure, but he sensed she was at a crossroads. For a moment, he allowed himself to hope that she might be the key to his escape. But hope was a dangerous thing in a place like this. Was he hoping for hope's sake? He had to keep his focus. Loyalty and betrayal were all part of this game. But could she be trusted to help?

As the fire crackled again, Grant closed his eyes. His mind was already on the move. Was he on the edge of some new possibility? The price of trust was steep in a land like this. For now, the cabin would be his prison. But he would bide his time. When the opportunity came, he would make his move. He had no choice. He decided, if he had to break every rule in his book to do it, then so be it.

CHAPTER VII

Tiny Fractures

The following morning, Grant was slow to wake. He lay still, listening the activity around his bunk. The first layer was the snap and crackling pops of the fire in the iron stove. Above that hum came the low whistle of the wind outside, its shrill cry seeping in through the cracks of the cabin's walls and doorway. Next, there was a sharp, echoing scraping sound. The repetitive drawing of steel against stone.

Grant opened his eyes and could see Riggs, the gang's enforcer, sitting on a nearby lower bunk sharpening his knife. The large man had thick, weathered skin and a permanent scowl etched into his face just like the scar crossing his forehead. He was the type of man who spoke only when spoken to Grant had learned. Even the smallest movements of this brute told him a great deal. There was something restless in Riggs, something that hadn't been there the day before.

Across the room, Finley, the youngest member of the gang, was sitting on a rickety chair near the door, his knees bouncing nervously. His hands were trembling slightly, a telltale sign of anxiety that Grant couldn't ignore. Finley wasn't cut out for this life. Grant could see it in the way he fidgeted, the way he looked over his shoulder every few moments, as though expecting someone to burst in through the door at any moment. The boy was out of his depth, and it wouldn't be long before he cracked under the pressure. When that happened, he would either run or betray the gang, and neither option would bode well for him.

And then there was Lillian. She sat off to the side, Grant's own rifle resting against the wall beside her, eyes unfocused as she stared at the fire. The way she held herself: so quiet, so still gave him the impression of someone who had long ago accepted an inevitable truth. Besides McCade, the rest of the gang did not treat her as an equal, but they never underestimated her. Grant perceived that Lillian was more than just the tough woman with a gun. There was a darkness in her eyes, a kind of weariness that suggested she had seen things most people couldn't even imagine. It was the same kind of weariness Grant felt sometimes, the kind that only came from surviving too long in a place where survival was the only rule.

Milton and Harries were seated at the card table, mugs of some hot beverage steaming in front of them. There were leant in towards each other whispering.

"We should've heard by now," Harries muttered. "What the hell's taking them so long?"

"The hell if I know. I'm sick of this waiting," Milton replied.

The door banged open and a gust of cold air blew in along with McCade. He slammed the door shut behind him. Seeing the two leant close at the table, He challenged them, "And what are we conspiring about?" His voice was low, but there was an unmistakable edge of anger in it.

Riggs, still sharpening his knife, didn't look up. Finley, however, glanced nervously at McCade before lowering his gaze again, his hands still twitching at his sides. Milton and Harries did not reply but stared back with blank expressions.

The lines on McCade's face were pronounced and Grant noticed that the man's temper had grown shorter, his patience thinner. There was a gnawing, predatory tension in his posture. It was as if the walls of the cabin weren't the only things closing in on him.

TINY FRACTURES

"Well? Spit it out you two," he barked.

"We're sick of waiting," Milton whined.

"We should've heard something by now," Harries added.

"Maybe they got delayed," Lillian's steady voice offered from her spot near the wall.

"Delayed? They should've been here days ago, Lillian! We shouldn't have to wait this long for *anything*," Milton snapped.

"We wait!" McCade yelled and threw his gloves against the rough-hewn cabin's wall. "We wait, period."

Grant remained still, observing. His eyes darted across each member of the gang in turn. The air was thick with tension, tension that had nothing to do with his own fate, but everything to do with the fracturing unity of the gang.

McCade's frustration was growing by the minute. He paced back and forth, clenching and unclenching his fists. He didn't care to wait either and it was clear that the constant pressure of the unknown was starting to wear on him. He needed answers, and he needed them now. The more the gang hesitated, the more he would push them.

"I don't trust them with that gold," Milton complained.

McCade stopped in his tracks, eyes flashing with a mix of disbelief and anger. "Are you stupid?"

Milton looked around, confused, "Huh?"

"Are, you, stupid? Why would you bring that up in front of the Constable?"

The words hung in the air, heavy and charged. For a long moment, it seemed like McCade might lash out and do something to break the fragile veneer of civility the gang had left. But then, something in his eyes shifted. The anger remained, but it was tempered by something else, something almost calculating.

"Yes, you are just stupid. Simple and stupid," he remarked.

"I ain't stupid. I'm following the plan. Soapy's plan. He's the boss, not you."

"There you go again. Stupid and more stupid. Soap ain't here. I am and he left me in charge, you mutt," McCade barked.

"Enough of this," Lillian's voice was low, dangerously calm. "We don't need this."

"And what the hell would you know?" McCade fumed. His voice was sharp, each word laced with the weight of his frustration.

Lillian didn't flinch, "We're criminals, not soldiers Jerry. We don't follow orders. We follow a plan. We break the law and we get paid to do it."

"You'll do what I say, when I say it."

"Or what?"

As McCade reached for one of the revolvers at his waist, Riggs stood up and said, "We're all in this together, Jerry," He moved toward McCade slowly. His massive frame cast a long shadow. His voice low, he said, "We've been through worse. Who cares what this guy heard? The law's not going to find us up here."

McCade looked up at Riggs, his face contorting with frustration. "You think I'm worried about the law? You think that's what this is about?"

Riggs didn't answer. His eyes stayed locked on McCade, as his massive form stood unwavering. The tension was thick enough to cut through, but Riggs wasn't backing down.

Grant watched the scene unfold with quiet attention. There was more to this stand off than just gold, and McCade knew it. Riggs knew it. The others did too, even if they hadn't put it into words yet. McCade was losing control. As the gang was starting to fracture under his leadership, Grant knew something had to give. What may once had been a well-oiled machine, working for a single goal, was starting to unravel. The cracks in their unity were showing.

As if he heard Grant's thoughts, McCade's eyes flicked down to meet Grant's. There was something in McCade's gaze that sent a shiver down Grant's spine.

"I'm not the one who's in danger here," McCade said, his voice low and cold. "You are."

Grant kept his face impassive, his jaw tight, "I didn't say anything."

However, inside his mind, Grant's thoughts whirled. Soap. Soapy. This wasn't McCade's gang, it was Soapy Smith's. He had heard the reports coming out of Skagway about the notorious conman and gangster who ran the criminal dealings across that dangerous Alaskan city. Gold and Soapy Smith. Whatever this gang was up to, it had to be significant. Grant was quick to conclude that they would have to escape back over the mountains into Alaska to complete the heist.

McCade's eyes narrowed, the silence growing between them. There was a shifting in the air, a momentary lull as if the world itself was holding its breath. Then McCade said, "Anything else we need to talk about?"

Finley chimed in and said, "We're out of wood."

"Then get some more!" McCade shot back. "You know what? The adults need to talk amongst themselves. Take the Constable with you. He can carry the wood for you. And, Finley, you take a rifle and keep it pointed on him the whole time. He does anything: shoot him."

"Shoot him?" Finley stammered.

"You heard me. Oh, and Grant? Leave the coat."

"What?" Grant asked.

"The activity will keep you warm enough," was McCade's taut reply. "Can't have you trying to run off. You better work quick."

Finley looked entirely uncertain as he looked for a rifle.

"For the love of all that's holy," Lillian said. "Take the Copper's one" and threw Grant's Winchester across the room at the younger man. "You know what? You boys can have your little chat. I'll keep an eye on them both."

"Suit yourself," McCade sneered and turned to face the other men. "The three of you sit down."

CHAPTER VIII

The Escape

When the cabin's door creaked open, the cold slapped Grant like he was a misbehaving child. He'd been out in the Yukon long enough to know the brutal sting of the wind, but without his Buffalo coat, the frigid temperature bit through the red serge of his simple uniform jacket to send a tremor down his spine. His teeth clenched as the biting wind found every gap in his clothing. He was exposed and vulnerable. He had to move. His survival depended on it.

Looking around the homestead, he could see the woodshed was nearby. Cut timbers and cords of wood were neatly stacked under its shelter. It was only a short distance away, but each step towards it felt as if the cold were stabbing him in the chest.

Lillian was ahead of him, stepping through the snow with quiet precision. Her breath was visible in the air, dissipating almost instantly, swallowed by the harsh wind that seemed to surround them. The rhythm of her steps was measured and deliberate and she didn't look back as she moved. Finley was trailing behind them, visibly shivering despite his heavy jacket. The young man's anxiety was obvious as he gripped Grant's Repeater carbine in his gloved hands.

Grant followed Lillian, his mind sharpening despite the cold. His numb hands were clenched tightly at his sides. The lack of his coat was a small but significant blow to his comfort, but the fact that he was still alive kept his focus steady.

They were headed out to collect firewood, the plan laid out by McCade's orders, but Grant had other ideas. He had to act fast, before the tension inside the cabin grew too tight for him to escape unnoticed. The more time he spent in the gang's presence, the more he saw their fragility. McCade's control over them was slipping, but that was no guarantee of success. This was his first and best chance, and he had to seize it before McCade could reestablish his control and clamp down on any further dissent.

The three of them trudged on, the crunch of their boots in the snow the only sound breaking the stillness. The area around the woodshed had seen enough traffic to leave the snow churned and trampled, making it easy to split and stack find wood for the fire. Grant's eyes darted over the terrain, noting the positions of the trees, the thick clouds overhead, and the distant peaks to their west. The mountains the gang would have to traverse to get back to Alaska.

The cabin became a snow-covered shadow behind them. He had to focus and stay calm. There was no room for mistakes. He could feel his heart pounding in his chest as adrenaline began to surge through his veins.

Finley stumbled slightly; his hand clutched the carbine to his side as he tried to catch his balance. His face was pale beneath the dirt and stubble, his lips pressed together as though he were trying to keep some kind of control over his nerves.

Lillian glanced over her shoulder toward Grant for a moment. "Ready to work?" she asked, and there was an edge of urgency behind her words.

Grant nodded curtly; his face grim. "Let's get to it."

"Finley," Grant asked quietly, "Is there a sled, or am I carrying the stacks myself?"

THE ESCAPE

The young man hesitated for a moment, looking back over his shoulder. His eyes were wide and filled with the same nervous energy that had Grant watched plague him since they had arrived. He pointed and said, "Over there."

"Right, got it," Grant replied.

As he moved to pull the sled over to the shed, he reviewed his plan. It was simple, but dangerous. If he got Finley out of the way, there was a chance he could get Lillian on his side. From there, it was a matter of stealing horses, breaking out, and getting as far away from the cabin as possible.

He would have to move fast. Lillian was a wild card, but if he could get her to trust him? If he could get her to believe in the possibility of escape, she would be invaluable. Finley, on the other hand, was the real problem. The blind loyalty of the boy to McCade was a liability.

While Grant pulled the sled through the thick snow to the woodshed, his breath came in short, sharp bursts. The cold stung at his exposed skin. He felt the gnawing hunger in his gut, the exhaustion that had crept into his bones, but none of that mattered now. He had a plan. And it would either succeed, or it wouldn't.

Grant glanced at Lillian. Her back was turned to him with her rifle nestled on her crossed arms. She looked across the valley and almost made Grant believe she was almost at ease. Almost. He suspected she was keenly aware of him as he began pulling split logs from the shed and piled them onto the sled.

Finely stood a little to one side, his eyes darting nervously between Lillian and Grant. His grip on Grant's Winchester uncertain with its continual shifting. Grant could feel the way the young man was on edge. His tension was an opening, and he knew that if he could just keep Finley distracted for a few moments longer, he could make his move.

"Finley," Grant called out, stepping toward him. The boy looked up, eyes wide, his mouth slightly open as though he were about to speak. "We're going to need more wood than just this. Can you help me load?"

Finley nodded quickly, stepping forward and was about to lean the rifle against the side of the sled. He caught himself, "Uh, no, I can't. You gotta do it. McCade said you do it."

"Fine, it's just so cold. The sooner we load this the sooner we can get back inside."

"Then, work faster. Go on!" Finley urged and pointed at him with the rifle.

Grant returned to the woodshed for another load. *Damn.* As he collected up another armful he was calculating the selection of wood in the shelter. They had all been split small enough to fit into the stove's grate. He picked up a short log. It was thick enough to do some damage, and light enough that he could swing it without too much effort. Returning to the sled with his next load, he waited for the right moment.

Grant saw Lillian's back was still turned. All he could hear was his heart pounding in his chest. He felt the rush of blood through his veins as he closed the distance between himself and Finley. As he took a few steps closer, he worried that the boy could hear the pounding of his heart. He slowed himself down, making his movements slower and more deliberate, as though he were doing as was told.

Dropping his logs onto the sled, he pretended to be arranging them for transport. He noticed Finely turn around, distracted by the wind creaking the branches of the trees. Grant chose to take his chance. In one swift motion, he grabbed the short, thick solid piece of wood and swung it toward Finley's head. The young man barely had time to react before the log crashed against his skull with a sickening thud. Finley's body went limp, dropping like a ragdoll into the snow. His rifle clattered to the ground with a dull thud.

Grant stood over him for a moment, his breath coming in shallow bursts. Behind him, he heard the lever action of Lillian's rifle as she racked a round into its chamber.

Grant raised his hands and waited a moment, but Lillian didn't speak.

"I'm going to turn around," Grant said. "Please don't shoot me."

THE ESCAPE

Lillian's eyes were colder that the environment. As she held her aim dead on him, Grant saw the eyes may be cold and assessing him, but they were not surprised. She didn't move to stop him. Instead, she gave him a silent nod, her gaze flickering over to the unconscious boy at his feet. She didn't ask what had just happened. She didn't have to. She understood.

"I'm taking his jacket."

Without any reply from her, Grant stooped down, his hands quickly working at the buttons on Finley's jacket. The jacket would be a necessity, Grant couldn't survive the cold without it. Stripping it from his unconscious form as quickly as he could manage, Grant threw it over his shoulders and buttoned it up. Next, he stripped Finley of his gloves and hat, and the revolver that was tucked into his waist. Leaving the boy unprotected and unconscious in the snow, Grant collected his Winchester from the snow by the sled.

Lillian stepped closer, her boots crunching on the packed snow. "What's your plan?" she asked him quietly, her voice tense.

"We steal horses," Grant replied, "and we get out of here."

She didn't hesitate, only nodded once, a brief but firm acknowledgment of his words. "Let's move," she said, her tone resolute.

"After you," Grant replied.

Not sparing a second glance at Finley's unconscious form behind him, Grant suspected this was a death sentence for the boy. Life in this gang would likely have led to the same end, only one that would be more gruesome and painful than this quiet death in the snow. There was no time for regret, his mind was already on the next part of the plan, getting the horses, getting away, and getting out. The two of them moved silently across the homestead. Lillian was leading the way as they approached the barn where the gang's horses were housed. The horses were their ticket out of here, if they could get them without alerting anyone in the cabin.

Sliding the main door open, Grant and Lillian entered the barn. The horses, restless inside the relative warmth of the building, snorted and shifted in their stalls. When Grant moved toward the nearest stall, Lillian hissed at him, "Over here. These two."

Grant joined her and found two horses had already been saddled. She pointed to a sturdy gelding, its coat thick with winter fur. Grant looked at her with surprise.

She replied, "No time. Questions can come later."

Grant nodded and slung his rifle across his back. He moved with the quiet confidence of someone who had ridden for years, his hands gentle as he untied the reins.

Lillian was already up on her saddle. Grant's heart pounded, but he kept his movements slow and steady. If the gang spotted them now, everything would fall apart. They would be trapped. Grant mounted the gelding swiftly, as he turned the horse, he heard her say, "Grab this line."

She was offering him one end of a rope that was tied off to the piles of other saddles stacked up on the floor.

Taking up the rope, Grant tied it around the pommel of his saddle. Urging his new mount forward with a soft click of his tongue. Lillian followed suit, her own horse snorting as it shifted its weight beneath her. They trotted out of the barn, dragging the pile of saddles behind them. There was no sign of anyone leaving the cabin. Without another look back, they rode away from the Homestead, the sound of their horses' hooves muffled by the thick snow beneath them. But they weren't free yet.

As they crested a rise, Grant could still see the dim outline of the cabin back in the valley. He knew McCade's gang would soon realize they were gone, if they hadn't already. Lillian and Grant had to keep moving and as much distance between themselves and the hideout as possible.

They had left the saddles somewhere in the forest behind them, enveloped in the snow. Even if the gang found them, they would not be on their trail anytime soon. This part of the escape was only the beginning. For now, they were free and breathing. And as McCade had pointed out, that was something.

They rode on into the bleak, snow-filled wilderness. As the day darkening around them, they couldn't afford to stop. Not yet.

CHAPTER IX

Down Skagway

It may have been late spring, but in Skagway, the Alaskan winter always lingered. The little town, at the tip of the Taiya Inlet, was nestled in a narrow valley between the mountains and the ocean. Once a forgotten outpost at the edge of the world, it now bristled with energy, waiting for the gold rush to either save it or destroy it. The green waters at the confluence of the inlet and the Skagway River reflected the noonday sun during this a brief series of sunny days.

    One of the few saltwater ports close to the Klondike goldfields, Skagway had been built in a hurry, a patchwork of hastily constructed wooden shacks, tents, and saloons. The main street, made up of dirt and gravel, was muddy and worn. The wind whistled down from the towering peaks of the Coastal Mountains, biting through the worn cloth of the miners' jackets and made the shadows feel colder than the already biting temperatures would suggest. Skagway's first settlers had dug into the wilderness like men trying to burrow into an earth that didn't want them. They had worked tirelessly, creating the town's rudimentary infrastructure and building what they needed to survive in this harsh environment.

THE DEAD HORSE TRAIL

There was no pretension in the town. It was a place of survival, of ambition, and of desperation. Some had come seeking their fortunes; others had come out of curiosity, pulled by the rumours of the gold-filled rivers far to the north. Every man and woman who stepped onto Skagway's muddy streets had the same thing in mind: wealth, and a future beyond the stony shores of the Alaskan frontier.

Skagway was at the very centre of the rush towards the Klondike. The hopeful had flooded in by the thousands, traveling from every corner of the globe they had only one goal: to reach Dawson City. There, the Yukon's gold waited like a dream to be grasped. However, between them and that dream lay unforgiving mountain passes and a treacherous journey that could make or break anyone. Before that journey, they had to navigate the predators lying in wait around the town, looking the fleece the naïve of whatever money could be taken.

As soon as a person stepped off their boat, they were greeted by the noise of the town, a mix of human voices, wooden carts, and the clatter of hooves on the street. The smell of horses, sweat, and the occasional waft of cooking meat hung in the air. The town was groaning with swift expansion. It was easy to see that something larger than mere survival was happening here.

Once the gold seekers flooded into town it had become a battleground. The swirling focal point of the chaos was Jeff Smith's Parlor. The small, whitewashed saloon had quickly become the beating heart of Skagway's social life. Its saloon doors swung open and closed, allowing the smoke and laughter from inside to spill out onto the muddy street, a signal to all who walked by that life here was wild, unpredictable, and often fleeting.

Inside Jeff Smith's, the atmosphere was lively, though rough around the edges. The wooden floors creaked beneath the shuffle of boots, and the walls were plastered with peeling advertisements for goods and services no longer available in town. The bar was polished, well-kept despite the dust that found its way in through the open doorway. The bottles behind the bar gleamed under the light of a few hanging oil lamps, their colours casting a warm glow over the faces of those gathered.

DOWN SKAGWAY

The Parlor was a place of refuge, a place to escape the brutal realities of the outside world. But it was also a place where deals were made, alliances forged and sometimes broken. And at the centre of it all, behind the bar or playing cards with whoever dared to challenge him, was Jefferson Randolph "Soapy" Smith.

A man with a sharp smile and sharper eyes, Soapy had built a reputation in Skagway. Not just in the Parlor, he was one of the town's most influential men. As a businessman, he knew the ins and outs of the town better than anyone, and he wasn't afraid to use that knowledge to his advantage. He had seen the gold rush bring in all manner of characters the honest, the dishonest, and some who were just in it for the thrill.

Soapy was a man of many talents. He was also a con artist, a hustler, and a showman. The kingpin of Skagway ran the town's most infamous gang of swindlers and crooks. He didn't hide his true nature. He lived out in the open, in full view of anyone who dared to cross him, and he was good at what he did. He had the gift of persuasion, the ability to make people believe that what he offered was too good to pass up.

It was said that Soapy could sell you your own boots and make you believe you needed to buy them back from him. His most famous trick had involved a rigged lottery: an elaborate ruse where customers would pay to enter and then, in the end, find out that the prizes they'd won didn't exist. But the allure of the game and the promise of winning kept people coming back, even when they knew they were being played.

The men and women who entered Jeff Smith's Parlor had come from all corners of the world, and many of them didn't know what they had walked into. Some came to drink, others to gamble, and still others to be entertained by the rough crowd of characters who populated the saloon. But those who paid attention soon learned that this was not just a simple watering hole. It was a crossroads for anyone with ambition, or anyone looking to make a quick fortune. It was where deals were struck, secrets were whispered, and where fortunes were won and lost.

Soapy Smith's presence in the Parlor was not incidental. Though he wasn't the official owner of the saloon, he was the one who ran the show behind the scenes. His influence spread beyond the walls of the Parlor, known as 'the real city hall', and it affected the entire town. He was the man who controlled the action, whether it was the illegal gambling rings or the underworld of cons and schemes that made the gold rush an even more dangerous place than it already was. For Soapy, Skagway was both a playground and a stage. A place where his charm and duplicity could run wild. He and his gang were everywhere, hidden in plain sight, working their scams like a well-oiled machine.

The town, for all its rough edges and lawlessness, was also filled with those who were just trying to make it through the madness. A small-time prospector could find himself walking into Jeff Smith's Parlor to try his luck at cards, his hopes pinned on an imagined fortune in the Klondike. Others would wander in, hoping for information on the best route to Dawson, only to find themselves entangled in a web of half-truths and half-deals, with Soapy smiling in the background, always two steps ahead.

At night, the sounds of the Parlor's piano would drift out onto the street, accompanied by the raucous laughter and shouting from the gamblers. But beneath it all, there was an undercurrent of tension. There was always a sense that the town was teetering on the edge of something much darker, and that it was only a matter of time before the gold rush would either lift Skagway to unimaginable wealth or swallow it whole.

For now, though, it was a town alive with hope and greed, a place where fortunes were made and lost as quickly as the tides that washed up against the shores. The streets were packed and only the shrewdest would see the gold rush through to the end. It was a place where dreams were born, and nightmares could be just as quickly realized.

Exiting the Parlor, a tall man pushed his way out the door, past the queue of hopefuls waiting to get inside. He adjusted his Boss of the Plains hat, with its centre right brim pushed up front and bound edge now perched a rakish angle. Puffing on a cheroot, he smoothed his moustache as he walked away from the saloon with purpose, newspaper in hand.

The narrow muddy street he walked along was framed by wooden boardwalks and rough-hewn buildings. The scent of fresh cut pine from the surrounding forests mixed in with the smoky haze of campfires, where people huddled close cooking their meals. A cacophony of sounds filled the air, the clop of horses' hooves, the chatter of miners haggling for supplies, and the clink of metal as prospectors carried their gear through the streets.

The shops lining the street sold everything from mining tools to food, clothing, and whiskey. Miners were in a hurry to stock up on supplies before heading out on the gruelling journey to the Klondike, and the man watched their frenetic rush in and out of the general stores.

Turning one corner, he approached a standalone wooden building. Small and rudimentary, not unlike the design of Jeff Smith's Parlor, a newly carved wooden sign hung above its door that proclaimed: 'Telegraph'.

A long queue of people was lined up outside of the storefront's door. They all waited for the brief opportunity to send a message out to their loved ones saying they were alive and prospering.

Walking with purpose, past the waiting patrons, the man turned down the side of the building and headed to its rear. Opening the backdoor, he ducked his head under the low lintel of the door and entered.

Inside the small back room, lit by blackened oil lamps, was a heavy rough table with a few chairs and a more refined roll top desk. On the desk sat a black Telegraph machine and seated at the desk, were a crossed pair of boots propped up on the desk's edge. They belonged to a well-dressed man with a heavy gold watch chain and a trim Mephisto beard. Reading the Skagway News, he put the paper down and considered the man who had just entered his lair.

"Texas Jack Vermillion. How are we doing today?"

"I can't complain, Soap. Busy-busy," the man replied over the sound of morse code coming through the thin wooden wall as a Telegraph machine beeped out its dots and dashes.

"You just missed the Reverend," Soapy Smith said.

"What's he at?"

"The usual, ministering and being all around good at sending more suckers my way," Soapy chuckled.

"Got a message," Texas Jack said, holding up a small slip of paper.

"Very funny," Soapy replied.

"No, really," he insisted, "I got a message."

"What? To send your dear mamma back home in Virginia? We don't do that TJ. That's the whole point. We do nothing. Every now and then I'll start hitting this and pretend it's some sort of incoming message for the assembled idiots on the other side of the wall paying five bucks a head. You know there ain't no real telegraph in this town."

Soapy tapped out a quick dot-dash-dot-dot sequence on the machine to illustrate his point. "See?"

"I know we don't," he replied, with no small sense of exasperation. "Soap! This message got carried over the Chilkoot from... there. From Dawson."

"Dawson! Well then, why didn't you say so? Dawson: hub of all things bright and shiny. What's the message?"

"Job success. Returning. Law chasing. Heading back. Job Two next. Wish us luck."

"That's it?" Soapy asked.

"That's the lot. Here's the paper outta Dawson too. Story on the robbery."

"McCade! Couldn't he be a little more descriptive?" Soapy asked as he snatched the paper from Texas Jack's hand. "Just a little more descriptive? That agitates me. It's agitating me Jack. Alright?"

"I know, I know it's frustrating," he replied and added, "I think he's being clever, coded, just in case someone intercepted the message."

"Of course it's frustrating! You saying I don't know that? Give'm a little more cash next time so I can get decent messages. Ain't nobody going to figure out what that message meant. He's giving the Mounties too much respect. Well-well, coverage in the local news. Swoon. So, that worked."

"It worked."

"When can we expect 'em back? When's payday for Soap Daddy?"

"Three weeks. Maybe four. Depends on the trail."

"Aggh! The bloody Dead Horse Trail. I ain't crossing that death trap, ever! Or you neither. Gold's a fool's errand. Attract it, I say. Don't go dig for it. Stealing it? Hell, that's even better."

"Sure beats working for a living."

"That's for damn sure. Have I shown you this new one?" Soapy set down the Dawson paper and demonstrated a sleight of hand trick for his minion with a set of cards. His deft fingers and mastery of the art was impressive.

"Pretty slick boss."

After pouring himself a whiskey, Soapy offered the bottle to TJ, with a pleased look on his face. "The Dawson gold, I gotta say, is one sweet caper. But I want that lockbox from the Log Cabin even more. Should be hundreds of thousands up there."

"They'll get it," Texas Jack reassured Soapy. He took a long pull from the bottle before continuing, "McCade and his gang are old army bastards. He's got a new one too, one who knows their explosives. They'll crack that nut. Them Mounties ain't gonna know what hit 'em."

"We run a racket. You, run a racket for me. Which I appreciate TJ," Soapy said. He gestured at the walls around him, "This may be a racket. But those Canadian bastards up there? That's the real racket! They're making cash hand over fist. Governments, I spit on 'em."

"I hear ya. They'll take the lot."

"They will, won't they? And then? That's the best part: who's gonna chase them after they knock the Log Cabin over? Nobody! I love that plan," Soapy laughed to himself and finished off his glass with a swift snap of the wrist. "Then, we're rich-er. Send Slim Jim in, will ya? I got a task for him."

"Texas Jack stood and tipped his hat to Soapy. "Door open or closed?"

"Ajar," Soapy said, with a Cheshire Cat's toothy grin. "You never know when opportunity may knock or just walk on in."

CHAPTER X

A Fragile Trust

The night was still, the wind conspicuously absent. For once in the last weeks, snow did not fall, and the cold did not feel as biting and relentless as it had. This respite from winter's typical cruelty made the world feel small to Grant. The soft crunch of their horses' hooves on the frozen earth the only sound they could hear. The forest around them was a black-and-white world after the late afternoon had slipped into evening.

Grant and Lillian rode side by side, their horses plodding forward, each step slow and laboured. The woman's face was pale beneath the weight of her fur-lined hood, her eyes narrowed against the cold.

Finley's heavy wool coat, a few sizes too small for Grant, had grown more uncomfortable over the past hours. His bearded face was weathered and creased from days in the sun and cold and darkened by the constant shadow of fatigue.

They had ridden without a break since their escape from the homestead the day before. The horses' pace had been slowed by the deep snow. Lillian could feel the weight of their shared exhaustion in every step, in every aching muscle. Her back hurt. Her legs ached. There was no rest when you were being hunted.

When they reached a small clearing in the woods, there was a slight rise in the land where the snow had settled into thick drifts. It likely had once been camp for others, now eerily lay empty and silent. The faint outline of a fire pit marked the centre of the area. Tall pines bordered the space, their branches heavy with snow. Under the trees, Grant could see neat piles of stacked wood, mostly untouched by the snow.

"We need to give the horses a break," Lillian said.

"You'll get no complaint from me," Grant replied. "A fire wouldn't hurt either."

The woman dismounted first, stiff from the cold and the long ride, and immediately moved toward the edge of the clearing, her eyes darting nervously from one side of the trees to the other. She needed to make sure no one was watching. She didn't trust this place, not in the slightest. But they had little choice.

The man followed her movements with his eyes, keeping a steady hand on his saddle as he swung his leg over his horse, the movement fluid despite his fatigue. He led their horses to a rope strung between two nearby trees. After checking the rope was still sturdy, he secured the reins to it. His gaze scanned the surrounding tree line, his instincts on alert.

As he arched his back and stretched, the cold made his body ache deep in the joints. But there was something more pressing than his own discomfort. Safety still felt a long way off. The fire pit would give them some warmth, but it wouldn't stave off the cold for long.

He set to work quickly, gathering logs from the neat pile that also held a surprising amount of dry kindling. He started the fire with practiced efficiency. The crackle of the dry wood as it caught was like a promise, a brief flicker of warmth in the vast emptiness of the night. But even as the fire began to burn, Grant felt the weight of the situation bearing down on him. He kept one eye on the woman, knowing Lillian was just as wary as he was.

She took a seat on an old log near the fire pit and leant her rifle beside her. Wrapping her woollen shawl more tightly around her shoulders, her cheeks were flushed from the cold. As her eyes scanned the trees, she hugged her arms to her chest, trying to hold onto what little warmth the fire gave her.

"No one's going to find us tonight," Grant offered.

"You sure about that?" she countered.

"I hope so."

"Hope?" she scoffed, then said, "I've got no time for hope. Hope's useless concept."

"Even if it's all we have?"

"Especially then," she insisted, frowning.

"Tonight may be only time can get some rest and warm up. While I'm not certain, I'll cling to my hope for now, thank you."

Grant's breath puffed in little clouds, mixing with the smoke from the fire. His mind was far away, somewhere back in the past. The fire was supposed to bring some small comfort, but his nerves remained on edge.

When he glanced at Lillian, he caught her gaze for just a moment before quickly looking away. Her expression was unreadable, as it always was. The lines around her eyes and mouth had deepened with fatigue. There was no softness in her face, only the hardness of someone who had seen too much, lost too much.

"Why did you help me?" he asked.

She didn't answer, her hands working methodically as she adjusted some of the burning wood. The fire crackled and popped, the only sound in the frozen stillness of the woods.

She looked up sharply, locking eyes with him, "I really don't know." she said, bitterness creeping into her voice.

"Having regrets?"

"I regret leaving Finley in the snow. Yeah. He was just a kid."

Her voice faltered at the end of the sentence, and Grant could hear the rawness in it. She didn't need to explain. He understood it all too well.

For a long moment, neither said anything. The silence stretched between them like the distance between two people who had learned to trust only the cold and the fire.

When Grant spoke again, his tone was steady as he asked, "You've been running for a long time, haven't you?"

THE DEAD HORSE TRAIL

She hesitated and he presumed she didn't want to acknowledge some truth. She looked as though she wanted to fight it and shut him down before the question could take root.

"Too long," she said quietly. She looked down at the fire, watching the orange and yellow flames lick at the dry wood, crackling with life. "I was never supposed to end up like this," she continued, her words spilling out now, uncontrollable. "I used to trust people. I used to believe that things could change, that I could have something real." She took a deep breath, her voice barely a whisper. "But, I can't. I haven't trusted anyone in a long time. Not even myself."

Grant looked at her, his gaze softening for a moment. He knew what she meant, even if she hadn't fully explained it. The world they lived in had no room for innocence, no space for the kind of trust that kept people safe. Everything was fleeting. Everything could turn on you in the blink of an eye.

"You don't need to trust yourself," he said after a pause. "You just need to trust that you'll keep going. That you'll survive. That's what matters."

His words were simple, but there was an unshakable certainty in his voice that made her want to believe him. She swallowed hard, blinking against the sudden heat in her eyes.

"And you?" she asked, her voice quieter now. "Do you trust me?"

His expression hardened, the mask slipping back into place. He looked away, his gaze settling on the horses, standing just beyond the firelight. Grant didn't answer her immediately, but she could see the tension in his posture, the muscles tightening across his shoulders.

"I don't know," he said, after a long silence, his voice quieter, as though he was speaking more to himself than to her. "What I do know is that right now, you're the only person who can help me survive. I think you know that's also true for you."

The words hung in the air between them, heavier than the night itself. Grant could feel the weight of his trust, as fragile as it was, and knew he wasn't ready to fully let go of the wall he'd built around himself.

"You're probably right." Lillian said. "They aren't going to catch up by tonight."

"Thanks for the vote of confidence," Grant replied and laughed.

"No problem," Lillian said, then broke into laughter herself.

"Quite the pair we make," Grant added.

"Quite," she agreed. "You're turning into a proper Outlaw: stolen clothes, stolen horse. Stolen guns."

"The rifle was mine, I only stole that back," Grant choked when he thought about the boy again. "I guess you can add murder to that list."

The fire crackled between them. At the edge of the clearing, their horses stamped their hooves in the snow, restless in the cold, but neither of them moved to tend to them.

"Tell me about the heist," Grant asked her, desperate to change the subject. "You robbed some gold in Dawson and then what? Escape back to Skagway and Soapy Smith?"

"Something like that," Lillian replied.

"What am I missing? McCade said he had a plan for me?"

Lillian sighed, "The Dawson gold was the first part of the plan. The first job. That was easy enough. It was the down day grab. Once the saloons closed for Sunday and after they had bagged up their week's take, it was all just sitting there for waiting us. Sacks upon sacks of gold. We hit every saloon and gambling hall along Front Street. As Dawson and your Mounties slept in their fort: one by one, we took it all."

Grant pressed her further, "And then?"

"We split up. McCade and us went one direction; and Murphy and his boys went in another to confuse the trails. We secured pack horses and sleds for the crossing and Murphy would meet us at the Homestead with the gold. Then we'd head for Alaska in force."

"Which pass? White or Chilkoot?"

"White. We'd spread out and cross as groups of Klondikers, returning with our gold. No one any the wiser."

"That's the first job, what's the second?"

Lillian hesitated, then continued, "We take White Pass. Hit the Log Cabin and take all the customs duties. We cross into Alaska and back to Soapy. Get paid, go live our lives somewhere else."

Grant whistled, "That's some plan. McCade figured he could use me to take White Pass?"

"I guess. He didn't tell us what he was cooking up for you."

"They've got a Maxim up there. He was planning to take the cabin under machine gun fire?"

"No, we were going to take everyone out with sharpshooters. One, by one, by one. Starting with the Maxim gun. Maybe he thought he could use you to get us in closer, so we didn't have to kill everyone first?"

Grant didn't answer. He simply stared into the flames, sifting through his thoughts. After he let out a slow breath, his voice was firm, "I have to warn them."

CHAPTER XI

The Burden of the Badge

The air inside the Log Cabin's cramped, dimly lit barracks felt thick. A single oil lantern flickered in the corner of the room. The soft glow cast dim shadows across the worn floorboards. Constable Dorsey leaned back in his chair, elbows resting on the edge of his desk, and stared at the map of the Klondike pinned to the wall. His gaze drifted over the familiar lines, marking trails and posts. To him, it was no longer the map of a lawman, a tool of order and duty, but a record tracking a series of obstacles, dead ends, and forgotten places. His eyes traced the routes from Dawson City, down the Yukon River to Bennett Lake and then White Pass. It was the route the future was travelling towards him.

The thick, bitter cold of White Pass had a way of creeping into every part of the post. No matter how many layers Dorsey donned or how tightly he clutched his cup of stale coffee, the chill persisted in settling deep into his bones. The wind outside howled as it always did, but tonight it seemed louder, angrier, as if the mountain itself was issuing its harsh verdict against the decisions he had made.

THE DEAD HORSE TRAIL

As the wind rattling the shutters of the station, he could hear the muffled sounds of activity from outside as the other Constables, his brothers in arms, went about their duties, unaware that their safety was being compromised. He listened to their footsteps on the snow, the sharp crunch of boots. It was just the sounds of this artificial order going about its business imposing structures on a world that in its usual, indifferent way cared little for the law.

Dorsey sat in the corner of the small office, his weary eyes fixed on the desk cluttered with maps, official reports, and stray notes from his colleagues. He turned his attention back to the task at hand: a single piece of parchment before him, covered in scrawled handwriting. Dorsey had just finished another message to McCade, outlining the details of White Pass's defences. His fingers hovered over the paper, the ink still wet, but he didn't dare hesitate. His thoughts were too jumbled, a whirlwind of guilt and necessity, each moment more difficult to reconcile

This final letter would seal the fate of the White Pass and all the men stationed here. It sat there now, the page burdened with the weight of his betrayal. He leaned forward, picking it up. The words burned through him now. It wasn't the first time he'd provided such intelligence. Dorsey folded the message with careful precision. Another fold, another step deeper into the lie. Another piece of his soul chipped away and sold.

Before sealing the letter, he pulled open his desk drawer. Inside, hidden beneath layers of official forms and dispatch reports, was a box of personal letters. His brother's letters. The ones that he had written, just before he died. It was here that Dorsey found himself most torn. When he thought about his brother's death, how helpless he had felt in the face of lawlessness, he found himself filled with the same fury that had led him to McCade's side in the first place.

His brother had been everything Dorsey was supposed to be: the idealistic Constable who believed in upholding the law, even in a place like this: where that law was a faint echo of its original promise. The system had failed his brother. And when Dorsey looked at his reflection, he saw a man who had given up on all of it.

"Justice?" Dorsey muttered to himself, the word feeling hollow on his tongue. "Justice doesn't exist in the Klondike. It never has."

When the floorboards creaked outside of his office door, they pulled Dorsey out of his thoughts. He snapped the box shut and shoved it back into the drawer, locking it with a swift motion. A knock sounded on the door, sharp and abrupt. He blinked and wiped his face, the exhaustion weighing on him harder than ever.

The door creaked open to reveal Constable Thompson, his young face flushed from the cold. Thompson was eager, full of the idealism that Dorsey could no longer recognize in himself.

"Dorsey," Thompson said, his voice brimming with excitement. "You hear the news from Dawson? A gold heist cleared out the town. Strickland wants everyone to report in. He thinks whoever did it might try to get out this way."

Dorsey didn't immediately respond. Turning in his chair to face Thompson, he could see the glow in the young man's eyes, the enthusiasm that permeated his every word. Just like his brother. Dorsey's pulse quickened as he met Thompson's gaze, as the statement was left hanging in the air. This wasn't a simple situation, and the answer wasn't straightforward. For a moment, his instincts flared. His duty, his deep, old commitment to the NWMP, told him to rally the men for a defensive stance. The very image of his badge, his place in the uniform, should have compelled him to rise up and meet this potential threat.

"Yes," he said, his voice calm, but hollow. "I've heard about the heist. Don't worry, Thompson, no one's coming here. We'll prepare, obviously, but we're ready for anything."

Thompson nodded, relief flooding his features. He trusted Dorsey, trusted the man who had been a guiding hand since his arrival at White Pass. The younger constable had no idea how fragile that trust was, no idea that the very man he relied on for guidance was betraying everything they stood for.

Thompson nodded, glancing toward the door, "Should we send word to the other posts? Just to make sure reinforcements are on the way?"

Dorsey fought the urge to recoil. He knew the truth: reinforcements wouldn't be coming. This was part of McCade's plan, allowing the NWMP to believe they had fortified the post and reinforcements were around the corner. When the gang struck, Dorsey would have ensured that there were no reinforcements to help. The temptation to warn the posts in Bennett Lake or Tagish to perhaps help in some way, was fleeting. Instead, he shook his head firmly.

"No need. We don't need reinforcements. We can handle this ourselves. I'll draft a message to the nearby posts though so they're aware." The words felt foreign on his tongue.

Thompson seemed satisfied, but there was something in his eyes that Dorsey didn't like. Was it a flicker of suspicion. Thompson wasn't stupid. He was just too green and idealistic to see the full picture. If he ever discovered the truth about Dorsey before McCade's attack, it would shatter everything.

The younger Constable exited the room and left Dorsey alone with his thoughts once more. As Thompson's footsteps faded into the background noise, Dorsey turned his gaze back to the letter on his desk. The message was simple. Straightforward. Information that would give McCade's gang an edge, detailing the vulnerabilities of the post. The hidden supply caches. The weak points in their defences. The posts where the sentries were most likely to be. The location of the money and the gold.

It wasn't just a message. It was a death sentence for those men. Dorsey stood up from his chair, his mind racing with the knowledge of what was coming. The betrayal felt like a weight on his chest, a stone too heavy to bear, but he couldn't undo what had already been set in motion.

At first, he had held a quiet conviction, the idealistic belief that the law could still be upheld. That the badge he wore still meant something. But every day in White Pass had chipped away at that belief, and after his brother's death at the hands of a murderer who was allowed to leave Dawson rather than be charged and hung? Everything he had believed in now meant nothing. The badge he wore no longer felt like a symbol of justice. It felt like a chain connected to the weight of his brother's expectations, dragging him deeper underwater. What would his brother think of him now? What would he say?

The questions were meaningless. The answer had already been written.

THE BURDEN OF THE BADGE

"Duty," Dorsey muttered to himself in agreement, his hand shaking as he clutched the letter. "Duty's nothing more than a chain."

Sweeping his Buffalo coat over his shoulders, he opened the office door and stepped outside. The cold air swept across his face and cleared his mind of its doubts. The future was now clearer than it had ever been. He was in too deep. McCade's gold, the promise of wealth and an escape from this posting was too tempting to walk away from. And so, he wouldn't. Doubts be damned, he would seize his freedom.

The relative quiet outside was palpable above the ceaseless wind. He could hear the rippling fabric of the flags flying above the post. The cold seemed to seep into his very bones, each breath a reminder of how far he had fallen. Dorsey made his peace with the man he had become. The law had failed and McCade's plan would succeed, and that was enough.

He would be free, in the end. Or so he told himself.

Dorsey's boots crunched against the snow as he walked across the yard toward the central log cabin that gave the post its nickname. It was where Inspector Strickland had been spending most of his time. The light from oil lamps inside flickered through its window. It was late in the evening, and the rest of the men were either on watch, or in the barracks. A few remained in the cabin, huddled around the stove, talking in low voices. The post was quieter than it had been in days.

Inside, finding Strickland sitting at his desk, Dorsey removed his hat and stood to attention. The older man was hunched over some paperwork, his glasses perched low on the bridge of his nose.

"Ah, Dorsey," Strickland greeted him without looking up. "At ease. Come, have a seat. We need to go over some things."

Dorsey stepped closer, pulling out a chair across from the desk. Strickland was a man of few words, and fewer still when something was amiss. Strickland's usual calm demeanour seemed strained.

"How are we looking?" Strickland asked, lifting his head. His eyes, sharp and calculating, met Dorsey's. "As you've heard, there was quite the robbery in Dawson. I've had reports, rumours really, that the culprits may pass this way during their escape."

Dorsey sat back in the chair, his hands resting loosely on his knees. He knew better than to downplay the situation, but he also couldn't afford to show too much fear or hesitation. There was too much riding on the next few days.

"We're holding steady, sir. Do we have any idea about who's behind the robbery?"

"None whatsoever, the usual whispers: Soapy Smith and his lot," Strickland replied.

"How do we know they're coming this way?"

"We don't, officially. If it is Soapy Smith, then the trail leads to Skagway. One way or another the trail inexorably leads to Alaska. No one is going rob that much gold and then sit it out in the Yukon."

"This is all rumour and whispers then?"

"Regardless, if it ends up being true: are we ready?"

"We've made improvements to the defences. The men are all aware of these rumours and are on edge. It's not high alert, but everyone's ready to respond if something happens. Patrols are covering all the usual routes."

Strickland's lips pressed into a thin line as he stared at Dorsey. "Ready is one thing," he said slowly, "How much money are we sitting on right now? How are our stores and supplies?" He paused for a moment, his voice taking on a sharper edge. "I know we've been doing our best. Yet, we can ill afford to be caught unprepared by this threat."

Dorsey felt a pang of discomfort. The question wasn't entirely about the money, it was about the position of trust he held in this post. Strickland had been growing more concerned with their state of readiness. Dorsey had been tasked with keeping track of all the supplies, including the customs duties that had been collected. There was far more money on post than most knew.

"We've got about five hundred pounds of gold and nearly a hundred and fifty thousand in cash and coin," Dorsey confirmed, lowering his voice. "We have enough rations and supplies on hand to hold us over for the next few months weeks. No one's going without."

67

THE BURDEN OF THE BADGE

Strickland's gaze narrowed, his brow furrowing, "Five hundred pounds and one fifty, you say? That's quite a sum, Dorsey. Quite a sum indeed," he repeated, as though tasting the numbers. "And where exactly is all that being held?"

Dorsey felt the weight of Strickland's gaze, as though the question was a slow trap being sprung around him. He exhaled quietly and leaned forward slightly, trying to appear unruffled.

"The gold and cash are secured in lock boxes in the weapons magazine. Everything's accounted for. I've made sure of it."

Strickland was silent for a long moment, his eyes locked on Dorsey's. There was no sign of the typical warmth in his face. Just a cold, hard assessment. "I'm certain you've got it all handled," he said finally, sitting back in his chair. "Still, I don't like it. That's too much to have laying around. We need to arrange to get those funds out of here."

Dorsey nodded in agreement, though his stomach tightened at the words. "I understand, sir. I have despatches to send down to the Bennett Lake post warning about the scenario. I can get some of their men to reinforce us and assist with an escort when we transport it out?"

Strickland gave him a hard, lingering look, as though trying to peer through the layers of Dorsey's words, to see the truth hiding beneath. The inspector sighed, smoothed his moustache and stood up. He walked to the small stove and poured himself a fresh cup of coffee.

"Make it so. Having some more rifles up here will help. They'll have to take it all back east overland. There's no way we send it out through Skagway. Feels too risky."

"Yes, sir. I'll make the trip down to Bennett Lake myself."

"Very well. I want a guard posted in the magazine going forward, Dorsey. Tighten everyone up. I don't trust this quiet we had the last few days. I certainly don't trust anyone who claims to have everything under control."

"Understood, sir. I'll handle it."

Strickland set the coffee pot down with a heavy clatter. Turning back to face Dorsey, his sharp eyes narrowed, "And Dorsey," he added, his voice quieter but no less intense. "I know you've got a lot on your plate. If anything happens? If there's even

THE DEAD HORSE TRAIL

the slightest chance we're compromised, it's not just my head that'll be on the chopping block. Make sure you're not overlooking anything."

Dorsey straightened, fighting the cold sweat creeping down his back. His throat constricted, but he kept his voice steady, "I'll make sure everything's in order, sir. You have my word."

Strickland gave a final nod, his gaze lingering on Dorsey for a moment longer than necessary before turning back to the fire. His final words hung in the air, "See that you do."

As Dorsey left the office, he couldn't shake the uneasy feeling that gnawed away inside. Could Strickland sense that something wasn't right? And more troubling still, could Strickland know that, for all of Dorsey's reassurances, the man tasked with keeping White Pass safe was the very one who had sold them out?

The questions burned in his brain as he walked past the Maxim gun position and down towards the stables. He had found his way out and would carry the letter to McCade himself.

CHAPTER XII

Betrayal in the Snow

McCade's boots crunched against the frozen earth as he stepped into the clearing near the woodshed. His eyes scanned the bleak landscape. The wind carrying with it the scent and bite of the winter's domination over everything he could see. His breath came in sharp, white puffs as he moved toward the body lying in the snow. His boots were heavy, caked in snow, but it was the weight of a betrayal that made the world feel heavy. Nothing in the world could match the icy grip of this moment.

Finley.

The youngest of the gang. Barely more than a boy, really. He had seen the fire in Finley's eyes when he first joined, a hunger for something greater, something beyond the rough life they lived. McCade had seen the kid grow into his role over the last few months, had watched him learn the ropes of a life that would chew up most man without hesitation. He could almost hear Finley's youthful laughter echoing through the trees, the way the kid used to joke about the life they had lived before, and how one day he'd find something better. But now, that dream was shattered. McCade had failed to protect him. Now, here he was, a lifeless heap in the snow under the grey sky.

McCade knelt beside him, a grimace of pain flashing across his weathered face. The snow around the boy's head was stained crimson, a stark blot against the whiteness of the world. He had seen death before, hundreds of times, but never like this. There were no comforting thoughts, no familiar rhythms to ground him; only this crushing silence and the bitter realization of how easily loyalty could be shattered, spread out across this snow like broken glass.

"Goddamn it," McCade muttered under his breath. His gloved hand hovered over the kid's lifeless chest, but he couldn't bring himself to touch him. It was too final, too permanent. He clenched his jaw, fighting the burn in his throat. "I'm gonna break bone in that Constable's body."

He stood slowly, scanning the horizon, the shadows of the trees closing in about him as though they too mourned the loss of one of their own. The forest around McCade seemed quieter than ever, the wind still, as though nature itself was holding its breath. It wasn't just Finley's death that twisted McCade's gut, it was the betrayal that came with it.

The sound of boots crunching on snow outside snapped McCade from his thoughts. He turned sharply when he heard the others approaching, his body instinctively going tense.

Milton, Riggs, and Harries trudged through the snow, their faces dark with a grim realization they needed to share. They had seen the body. They knew what it meant to McCade.

"Grant's gone," Harries said, his voice low, almost like a growl. "And Lillian. Both of 'em. Took two horses."

McCade didn't look up from Finley, he asked, "What else? Why aren't you saddling up the horses?"

Milton chimed in, "Saddles are gone. They took all of 'em."

McCade felt his stomach drop. The horses and all the tack had been secured in barn. Lillian had checked on them herself. Now, she was gone. The saddles were gone. And so was Constable Grant. The goddamn lawman had played them all for fools, and Lillian had sold them out.

"Lillian." McCade's voice was strained, colder than the air around them. "She turned on us."

Milton nodded grimly, "She was too quiet, McCade. Always watching. It don't surprise me none."

"Damn it all." McCade gritted his teeth and turned his eyes toward the trail leading west, toward the distant mountains. "I should've seen it." They were already well ahead, he thought, those two. The stolen horses would put miles between them before long.

"What do we do now?" Harries asked, his voice trembling just slightly.

Fear had crept into his words, and everyone could sense the hesitation in the air. They all felt it, even if they didn't say it aloud: this wouldn't just be about revenge anymore. This was about McCade.

McCade's gaze hardened. He wiped his hand over his face, his fingers rough with the cold. There was work to be done. There was blood to be spilled. "We find them. We don't stop until we do," McCade said, his voice like steel.

Milton's breath was ragged in the freezing air, "You're sure we can catch 'em?"

McCade's gaze sharpened, the anger in his eyes was unmistakable. "No one betrays me and lives. We'll hunt 'em down like dogs. Grant's gone too far. Lillian? Well, she'll wish she never crossed me."

The three men exchanged uneasy looks, but none of them dared question McCade. They all knew what he was capable of when pushed to the edge, and they had seen firsthand how he dealt with betrayal. They knew what he was capable of when pushed too far. The cold wind returned with a whistle through the trees, as if the very wilderness was urging them on, urging them to seek justice, and claim their revenge.

"Follow their tracks, they aren't dragging them saddles too far," McCade ordered them.

The snow crunched beneath their snowshoes as they began their search, their eyes scanning the ground for the traitor's trail. As they hunted for the saddles buried in the snow, all McCade could hear was the pounding of his own heartbeat, the rush of blood in his veins, and the promise of the violence that was to come.

It had taken a few hours, but as McCade had foreseen the saddles had indeed been dumped. Had the weather or wind been against them, they never would have been found. The Yukon had paid McCade and his gang the ultimate favour: luck.

By the time they returned the frozen saddles to the barn, darkness had been seeping across the sky and night was about to descend. However, the Homestead they returned to was no longer empty. The rest of the crew had arrived. With them they brought more rifles, fresh horses and the gold.

The cabin's door creaked open as McCade strode inside, his boots heavy on the wooden floor. The room was thick with the smell of new sweat and fresh tobacco smoke. The stove's flickering fire shone on the worn-out faces of the reinforcements. They were a rough bunch, seasoned men with hardened eyes. They kept their weapons close and stayed near the piled burlap sacks which they had heaped against the cabin's back wall.

McCade's gaze sharpened as he spotted the stocky man standing between him and the sacks.

"You're late, Murphy," McCade muttered, eyeing the newcomer warily.

"We was delayed," he replied, wiping dirty hands on his pants.

"Is that my gold?"

"You mean Soapy's gold? Yeah, right there," Murphy motioned to the sacks. "We need to move McCade and finish the plan."

McCade's eyes flickered to the gold, his heart racing at the sight of it. His mind was on revenge, though, not treasure.

"I don't care about the plan," McCade growled, his hand tightening on the grip of his revolver. "We got traitors to deal with. I'm not leaving until I find 'em."

A silence fell over the cabin, the tension had in an instant grown palpable between the two leaders. The new arrivals exchanged uneasy glances.

"You need to listen, McCade," one of the newcomers said. It was a scarred sharpshooter named Clement. "Traitors or no, this ain't the time for a reckoning. We stick to the plan. Like Texas

Jack told us and Soapy wants. After that, I'll come back to this godforsaken land and help you, but not now."

McCade's eyes flickered to Clement, with a fury, but it was Murphy who spoke up again.

"We're not sticking around. We make for Alaska. We stick to the plan," Murphy's voice was unyielding as he added, "These traitors of yours will have to wait. We're getting out of here with that gold before the law shows up, or worse."

McCade stood motionless, considering his next move. The weight of the gold piled against the cabin wall was tempting, but the gnawing urge for retribution burned hotter. He clenched his fists, then slowly released them, eyes narrowing.

"You think you can stop me?" he growled as his hand twitched on the grip of one of his revolvers.

"We'll stop you," Clement said, his long rifle aimed squarely at him now. "One way or another. We're not your gang. Don't forget that."

"If you don't want this payday anymore, then walk away now," Murphy added.

McCade's gaze shifted from Clement to Murphy, then across the others in the cabin. His anger flared, but the reality of the situation sank in. He had a choice: chase revenge and lose everything or stick to the plan and live to fight another day.

With a sharp exhale, he let go of his grip on the still holstered gun. "For now," McCade said, his voice filled with menace.

Murphy nodded, "We all want to survive, McCade. And get paid. Let's keep it that way."

The stove's fire crackled as McCade walked back to the door, his eyes dark with fury and his steps measured. The plan would remain in place, but something told him that he was not far away from the trail of those who betrayed him.

Stepping back into the cold, he slammed the cabin door behind him. Looking to the sky, he filled his lungs before screaming up to the heavens with all of his rage.

CHAPTER XIII

An Unlikely Messenger

Grant urged his horse onwards through the crisp morning. The gelding grunted softly beneath him as they climbed through the foothills. The trail ahead was narrow and winding, the earth frozen solid beneath their horses' hooves, the jagged outlines of mountain peaks barely visible in the pale light.

Lillian was just behind him, her horse, a dark chestnut mare, moved with a practiced grace through the rough terrain. She was quieter than usual, her eyes distant, as if lost in thought. Grant didn't mind the silence. It was practical. He was used to isolation; it was in his blood, after all.

They had been riding for hours, moving swiftly towards the mountains and eventually the trail to White Pass. They couldn't afford to waste time, and the snow-covered trail offered few opportunities for rest. McCade's gang was still out there, trailing them, just as dangerous and ruthless as ever. Grant's mind raced with the urgency of their situation. White Pass had to be prepared. He had to warn the post.

Every step they took felt like a race against time. Grant was driven by duty, the weight of his responsibilities pressing on his

THE DEAD HORSE TRAIL

shoulders. He knew what McCade's men were capable of, and what they intended to do at White Pass. There was no time for hesitation. The lives of everyone at the post depended on him getting there in time.

As for Lillian, Grant still wasn't sure where she stood. Her help had been invaluable in their escape, but he held many unanswered questions about her motives. The doubts gnawed at him. He couldn't help but wonder: what did she want from this? Why had she helped him escape the gang only to come this far, so deep into the wilderness, without any clear explanation? It didn't make sense. He wasn't sure if he could trust her, but in the end, she was the only ally he had. He knew he had to keep his guard up. It wasn't just her past that worried him. It was the way she carried herself now. It was the ease with which she adapted to the uncertainty of their situation.

With only brief stops to water the horses and take in what little sustenance they had, the constant rhythm of their horses' hooves against the frozen trails was all that kept Grant grounded. His eyes darted over the landscape, searching for any sign of movement. They had not encountered McCade's men yet, but he knew they were out there. The gang wouldn't give up that easily.

"We need to push harder," Grant muttered, his voice low and urgent. "They'll be coming after us."

Lillian looked up at him, her gaze calculating. "You're not wrong," she said softly, "but if we push too hard, we'll wear the horses out. We don't have the luxury of a fresh mount."

Grant didn't reply. He didn't have the luxury of time either, but she was right. They had to pace themselves if they were going to make it to White Pass. They needed to be sharp, ready for anything. His mount's hoof struck a rock hidden beneath the snow, sending a sharp jolt up Grant's spine. He gritted his teeth, holding onto the reins tightly to steady himself. The horse whinnied nervously, but he patted her neck reassuringly.

Lillian's horse also faltered for a moment, but she quickly righted the animal and urged it forward. "This snow is getting worse," she observed.

Grant nodded, scanning the trail ahead. They were still a long way from White Pass, and the closer they got, the more dangerous it would become. Grant's eyes caught sight of something in the distance: a figure on horseback, traveling at a steady pace with another pack horse behind them. Coming from the opposite direction, the man was dressed in rough, weather-worn clothes, with a wide-brimmed hat pulled low over his face. His horses were sturdy, their coats matted with dirt and snow, but they appeared fit, well cared for and strong.

Grant slowed, assessing the stranger. The man was riding alone, which made him an anomaly in these parts. Most travellers kept to larger groups in these conditions, especially with rumours of outlaws lurking. There was something about the man's steady posture and the way he handled the reins that intrigued Grant. He didn't seem afraid, and there was a quiet confidence in his movements. The deliberate ease suggested vast experience.

"We've got company," Grant warned and pointed ahead.

Lillian caught sight of the man too and slowed her mare to a stop beside Grant. Her eyes narrowed, and her lips pressed into a thin line. "Who do you think that is?" she asked, as her hands darted to check her rifle.

Grant shook his head. "I don't know, but we'll find out soon enough. Stay alert," he warned.

Lillian shot him a look that Grant couldn't quite place. Was it frustration? Annoyance? Maybe both. She didn't argue, but he could feel she didn't like being ordered around.

The stranger drew nearer, and Grant's instincts told him this rider had the air of someone who knew exactly where he was going, what he was doing, even if it didn't make sense for a civilian rider to risk being alone in the wilderness.

When the man was close enough, he pulled his horses to a stop with a smooth, practiced motion. His mount shifted about beneath him as he offered a polite and knowing smile.

"Buenos días," the man said and tipped his hat. His warm voice carried a faint accent that Grant couldn't place. He seemed unaffected by the cold or the harshness of the terrain. Grant studied him for a moment. There was something in the way the man looked at them, as if he was sizing them up just as much as they were him.

"Morning," Grant responded with a nod, his eyes scanning the man carefully. "You coming from White Pass?"

The stranger raised his eyebrows in mild surprise but didn't seem offended by the direct question.

"Si. Been over the Pass. It was a long ride," he said. "All the way from Mexico."

Grant's brow furrowed. Mexico? A long ride, indeed.

Lillian's eyes narrowed suspiciously. "Mexico?" she asked, voice laced with doubt. "You rode all the way from there?"

The man nodded, seemingly unphased by her incredulity. "I've been traveling for a year? Maybe more now?" he explained, his voice calm. "Made my way up through California and then heard about the gold. Crossing these mountains was not so easy. Yet, if you know where to look, the land gives you what you need."

Grant exchanged a glance with Lillian, who was still eyeing the man with scepticism. He couldn't blame her. A Mexican rider, alone in the northern frontier, was unusual to say the least. Something about the man's calm demeanour intrigued him.

"What's your business out here?" Lillian pressed, still uneasy.

"I'm riding to Bennett Lake, then onto Dawson City."

"You and every other idiot in the world," Lillian's reply was sharp.

Grant studied him, trying to gauge the truth of the stranger's words. He didn't like the idea of getting too close to anyone in their current situation. However, the man had travelled a long way. Maybe he could help them.

"My name's Grant. Bennett Lake, you say?"

The man's smile was slow, almost knowing. "Si, I'm Jorge," he said, not offering his hand, but his tone was friendly enough.

"You crossed at White Pass. You know the Police up there?"

"Si, the Mounties. Funny name: Mounties."

"Mounties, that's right. They have a post at Bennett. If I gave you a message, could you give it to them?"

Lillian's suspicion flared. She crossed her arms, glancing sideways at Grant. "What makes you think we can trust him with that?"

AN UNLIKELY MESSENGER

Grant held up a hand to defuse the tension. "We don't have time to be choosy. If he's willing to carry a message, I can't pass it up."

Lillian was silent for a moment, her eyes flicking back to the man. Her stance remained defensive, but there was no denying the practicality of Grant's point.

"Is it important? A matter of life and death?" Jorge asked.

"Yes, it is." Grant replied. "I can't offer you any money, but you'll save lives."

"Well, if that's the case then, Si," the man said with a shrug, the faintest glint of approval in his eyes. "I'll get them your message."

Grant took a deep breath, weighing his options. The man had a solid presence, and though his story was hard to believe, there was no denying that he had the knowledge to help them. And right now, the risk of trusting him seemed like the lesser of two evils.

He broke the silence first, "You don't want anything in return? No reward? No payment?"

Jorge leaned forward slightly, resting his hands on the reins. "I've seen too many men chase gold. Gold that isn't theirs to take. Gold that only brings more death, more hunger. I'm not here for that. I'm here because of duty."

"Duty?" Grant's voice softened with a mix of curiosity and suspicion. "You've crossed miles of hostile territory for duty?"

"Si," Jorge said, his voice unshaken. "Duty is something that guides me. Where I come from, we believe in 'honrar'. It's the measure of a man. It's all I have and all you have. You strike me as a man of honrar. I am honoured by your confidence in me: su confianza en mí me honrar. You say this message is important. If I can do the thing, no matter how small, then I will."

Grant didn't answer immediately, letting the weight of Jorge's words sink in. There was something about the man's calm demeanour. The dedication in his eyes didn't feel like the bravado of a drifter or opportunist.

"You believe in the law, then?" Grant asked, his voice quieter now.

Jorge met his gaze with a solemn nod. "The law, yes. Not just the law of men. The law of the land, too. The law of God. The one that cannot be bent or broken, no matter how much gold is in your pocket. The law of what is right. What is just."

Grant exhaled slowly, rubbing the back of his neck. "The law of what is just," he repeated. "I've been trying to hold onto that for a long time."

Jorge's eyes softened, a faint trace of understanding flashing across his face. "I know what it's like to lose your way. To be in a place where the rules no longer, how you say: fit? Sometimes, duty to something greater than ourselves keeps us steady. If you believe in what you're doing, then I believe in helping you."

"Even if you don't know me?" Grant's voice was edged with something approaching vulnerability.

"Especially because I don't know you," Jorge said. He gave a small smile, shaking his head, "If I were to ask, what drives you? Would you have an answer?"

Grant hesitated. It wasn't a question he was used to answering. It wasn't even a question he'd considered.

"I don't know," he admitted. "I guess, I guess I keep going because there's no other choice. My duty. For honour."

Jorge smiled, his eyes softening as if he understood all too well. "Then that is enough, I think."

For a moment, two men bound by duty to something greater than themselves shared an understanding in the wild.

Grant nodded slowly, the weight of his own burden shifting just slightly. "You'll carry the message because it's the right thing to do. Thank you."

Jorge tipped his hat and smiled, "Oh, está bien. The right thing to do."

And with that, the deal was struck. Grant looked at Lillian, who seemed to be fuming in silence, her distrust obvious but she held her tongue.

"Alright," Grant said. "Here's what I need you to say."

Jorge shook his head and reached into one of the saddlebags behind him. He removed a small leather-bound journal, with a pencil sticking out of the folds of its pages.

He held it out towards Grant and said, "Messages are much better written down."

CHAPTER XIV

Blood in the Snow

The reformed gang was cutting through the Yukon's stark landscape like a knife, slicing their way through the thick snow with relentless energy. It was powered by gold and the prospect of their payday at the journey's end. Their horses' hooves created a steady rhythm as the gang moved in near silence.

The wilderness stretched out around them, unforgiving and cold, the foothills and mountains ahead looming larger with every hour of their advance. White Pass was their destination, but there was more than just the impending assault on the NWMP post on McCade's mind.

The tension between McCade and Murphy had been building over the past days. The cracks in their fragile alliance more noticeable with every passing day. McCade's leadership and judgement had been questioned. The few loyalists could not help but notice how Murphy grew more resentful of McCade's decision making daily. The once steady leader had become more erratic in his actions, his judgment clouded by something darker. McCade had seen it coming, but even now, the speed with which things were escalating pointed to an inevitable outcome.

THE DEAD HORSE TRAIL

The gang rode in loose formation, with McCade at the front, his steely gaze fixed firmly ahead. He had disposed of his old jacket, and in its stead, he now wore Grant's discarded Buffalo coat. Behind him, Murphy rode a little to the left, his posture stiff and unnerving. McCade could feel the eyes of the gang on his back, but he didn't care. His mind was on the man beside him, once a close confidant.

McCade slowed his horse, the others following suit, until they were all nearly still in the snow. He pulled his reins tight, forcing his horse into a small circle, turning to face Murphy directly. The moment had come. His patience had run thin, and he was no longer willing to let this fester any longer.

"Murphy," McCade called out his voice was harsh and full of annoyance. "We need to talk."

Murphy didn't reply, his face hidden beneath the brim of his hat. The rest of the gang fell silent, eyes darting nervously between their leader and the second-in-command.

McCade needed to confront this now. He needed to remind Murphy who was in charge out here on the trail. He needed to remind the others as well.

"Murphy," he repeated, this time louder. His voice was thick with authority, "I'm talking to you."

Murphy finally turned his gaze to meet McCade's, his expression unreadable. The air between them felt heavy, charged with a tension that neither man was willing to back down from.

"I don't want to talk," Murphy said, his voice flat but with an undertone of something darker. "I think we both know what this is about."

McCade's lips curled into a sneer. "Do we now?" he asked, his voice dripping with venom. "What's your problem, Murphy? You've been acting like a damn liability these past few days. I don't know what's gotten into you, but I'm not going to let this go on any longer."

Murphy's lips tightening and the grip on his reins hardened. The other gang members watched in silence, sensing the storm that was about to break.

"I'm the liability?" Murphy's voice was filled with contempt. "I've finally realized what you really are, Jerry. A tyrant. A man who'll throw anyone under the wagon for his own survival. I've had just about enough of it."

McCade's jaw clenched, the muscles working beneath the skin as he held back the surge of anger rising within him. He needed to push this. Tip it over the edge. They may be close to their goal; but it wasn't entirely his goal anymore.

"You don't know what you're talking about," McCade said, his voice tight with frustration. "You're nothing without me, Murphy. Nothing but a damn shadow. If you think you can lead this gang, if you think you've got what it takes, then you're more of a fool than I thought."

Murphy's eyes locked with McCade's, and for a moment, there was nothing but silence. The wind howled around them, the snow swirling in the air, but neither man moved.

"I can do a hell of a lot better than you," Murphy said, his voice cutting through the silence like a knife. "You're not fit to lead anymore. This revenge you want? It's made you weak."

McCade's face twisted in a scowl, the anger boiling just beneath the surface. "You want to challenge me?" he asked, his voice low and dangerous. "You think you can control this gang?"

Murphy didn't flinch, his gaze was unwavering as they looked into each other's eyes. He said, "I'm not afraid of you."

Without another word, McCade reached for his sidearm. His hand moved so quickly that it was almost a blur. The cold steel of the revolver gleamed in the pale light of the afternoon. The gang was frozen in place, too shocked to react. No one expected this, no one expected McCade to go this far. Murphy had not even reached for his sidearm.

"Typical McCade," Murphy said with a shrug of his shoulders. "A snake to the end."

"Time to say goodbye," McCade muttered.

The shot rang out, breaking the frozen silence like thunder. The report echoed outwards across the snowy plains until it was swallowed by the endless snow.

Murphy crumpled out of his saddle. As he fell from the horse, a thick spray of arterial blood plumed out in a wide spray from his neck, staining the white snow beneath him. His body hit the ground with a dull thump, the life draining out of him as he gasped at his throat.

McCade didn't flinch, his hand still held the smoking revolver, his face as cold and expressionless as ever. He looked down at the body of his former right-hand man, the blood spreading out like a dark wreathe around him. "Anyone else have a problem with my leadership?" McCade asked them, his voice cold as ice.

Clement, the sharpshooter, dismounted and walked toward Murphy's body.

McCade's eyes locked onto him, and he barked, "Leave him!"

Clement raised his hands, "I'm taking his gun. He owed me."

McCade looked around. The gang was reeling from the sudden, brutal execution. His voice cut through the air, snapping them back to attention, "We're moving forward. There's no room in this gang for second-guessing. We're going to White Pass, we're taking what we came for, and we will get revenge on them two traitors. They insulted me. They killed one of you. Don't forget that. You got me?"

The rest of the gang, still in a state of shock, nodded their heads. They knew better than to question McCade now. His power had been solidified with Murphy's death, and they all understood the message.

No one was going to stop McCade. No one. He turned his revolver back on Clement. He warned him, "Take the gun. Just you remember when we're out of Skagway: you work for me. We clear on that score?"

Clement, hands still raised, begrudgingly agreed, "Yeah, I got it plenty clear."

McCade holstered his revolver and said, "Get on with it then."

Riggs, Milton and Harries exchanged grim looks with each other. They didn't say a word but instead urged their horses forward. The rest of the gang rode on, falling into line behind their leader and his three captains.

At the front of the column, McCade's expression was grim and resolute. The assault on White Pass was no longer just a robbery, it was personal. His gaze remained fixed ahead as the cold winds whipped around the abandoned body of Murphy, who was left behind to freeze in the snow.

CHAPTER XV

A Traitor on the Trail

The sun hung low in the sky, just cresting over the distant peaks of the Coastal Mountains. Grant squinted as he scanned the trail that stretched ahead, a ribbon cutting its way up through the white until it disappeared over Turtle Mountain. He and Lillian had made good progress through the Tutshi Valley since they had met Jorge, but they still had kilometres to go before they could feel any real sense of safety. McCade's gang could be anywhere, and the thought of them catching up was a constant, gnawing concern.

Lillian, her face set and hard, had remained largely silent since their last conversation. Grant found her difficult to read, but now, with danger so close, there was something in the way she kept her distance, both physically and emotionally which made him uneasy. The unease had only deepened since their encounter with Jorge. She seemed to be struggling with something, perhaps doubt, perhaps regret, but Grant didn't pry.

Their journey this leg had been long, and Grant knew they would need to find shelter before nightfall. His mind churned with what lay ahead. The unknowns that seemed to multiply with every turn, every new patch of snow. *Obstacles make life interesting*, he thought to himself. McCade's gang wasn't the only threat they had to worry about out here. Just as he was about to speak and break the gulf of silence between them, a figure emerged from around a bend further up the trail.

The man on horseback was riding steadily toward them. At first, Grant thought little of it, another traveller, perhaps? As the rider drew nearer, something about him stood out. The man wore a familiar broad Buffalo coat and peaked fur cap. He was a Mountie.

As the distance between them closed, Grant could hear the horse's hooves cut through the snowy trail with an eerie, rhythmic sound.

Grant slowed his horse. Lillian did the same, her expression unreadable as she observed the rider's approach. She said nothing, but Grant could sense her tension. It was the look of someone who didn't trust a man in uniform, himself included.

Once the rider drew within speaking distance, he reined his horse to a stop. The mounted Constable sat well in the saddle, his posture was rigid and unyielding. The man was tall, with dark hair and a strong, angular face. His eyes were cold, calculating. He scanned their movements, looking for any hint of a threat.

"Can I help you?" he asked in voice used to commanding authority.

Grant, his hand held up in greeting, said, "Yes you can! I have to say: you're a sight for sore eyes. I'm Constable Grant, from the Tagish Post. Where are you headed?"

The Constable regarded Grant with a measured glance, taking in his plain clothes and the lack of uniform that could mark him as a fellow lawman. "I could ask you the same thing. A Fort Selkirk Constable, you say? Out of uniform?" he countered, his voice clipped but not unfriendly.

Grant's gaze became focused. The man's tone seemed casual, but something in the way he spoke didn't sit well with him.

"I'm on official business," he replied. "My coat was left behind. Circumstance." Grant unbuttoned his stolen coat to reveal the red serge of his uniform jacket beneath. "What about you? Constable?" he asked, trying to keep his voice steady.

The other man shifted slightly in his saddle, his hand brushing against the sling of the rifle strapped to his back. "Dorsey," he replied, his eyes flicking briefly to Lillian, who was studying him with a pointed intensity. "I'm headed to Bennett Lake. What's this all about Grant?"

"There's a gang after us."

"Is this about that Dawson gold heist?"

"Yes, they're planning an attack on the Log Cabin. I'm trying to get ahead of them to warn the men there."

Dorsey's gaze never wavered when he said, "We've heard. There's no need for alarm. We're more than prepared."

Grant felt a new flicker of doubt. He had no reason to doubt Dorsey, but there was something about the man's words that felt off. The lack of urgency, the dismissiveness. He wasn't just downplaying the threat; he was undermining it.

Dorsey added, "You can spare yourself the ascent, Grant. It's a long ride to White Pass and these trails are hardly safe this time of year."

"You sound confident," Grant said, studying him more closely now. Dorsey's calm, almost dismissive tone didn't seem to match the gravity of the situation. 'You're part of the garrison at White Pass?" Grant asked, still eyeing Dorsey closely.

Dorsey shifted in his saddle again, but his expression didn't change. "That's right. I'm the Quartermaster," he said. Dorsey gave a tight smile, the kind of smile that didn't reach his eyes. "It's my job to keep things under control," he added. "And I do it well."

Grant took another moment to study the man. His posture was rigid, disciplined. Perhaps a little too disciplined, even guarded.

"What takes you to Bennett?" Grant asked, his suspicion growing by the second.

"Provisioning, not that it's any of your affair." Dorsey's smile was slight. There was a twitch at the corners of his lips, before he added, "Carrying despatches, the usual. All routine."

Grant felt a flicker of something dangerous in the pit of his stomach. The conversation, though polite on the surface had become a game of cat and mouse. There had been rumours, whispers really from some of the men out of Dawson that there were traitors in their midst. Constables who fed information to the highest bidder. Was Dorsey one of them?

"Good, I've already sent them a message to warn about the attack and send reinforcements. If you can follow up with them on arrival-"

"Why would I do that?" Dorsey shot back. When his gaze flicked to the side for a moment, Grant caught the briefest twitch of unease. It was subtle, but it was there. For just a moment, the facade of confidence had cracked. "Are you presuming to give me orders?"

"You're not worried about the gang?" Grant pressed, his tone growing more pointed. "Their leader McCade is ruthless. What about the men at the post? They're vulnerable. If he knows anything about the post's defences, everyone is at risk."

Dorsey's expression hardened for just a moment, before his easy smile returned. "McCade won't find White Pass an easy nut to crack. He's been chased off before. The post is more than prepared." His voice had become even more dismissive.

When his hand twitched near his revolver's holster, Grant's instincts flared. There was something dangerous in Dorsey's response, an aggression that hadn't been there before. The growing tension between them was palpable. Inside, Grant's suspicions were screaming with alarm. Dorsey's response didn't sound like a man stationed at a posting that was preparing for a potential siege. When Dorsey glanced toward Lillian, his gaze lingered a moment too long. For Lillian, it was the last straw.

"Bullshit," she said. "McCade's never gone after the Log Cabin before."

Dorsey turned to Lillian, "And how would you know that, Miss?"

"Spare me the Miss. I know because I was in the gang. We've never hit you once."

Grant was quick to back up Lillian's lead, "I'm afraid I can't let you pass. Not until I'm sure we're on the same side."

Dorsey's hand drifted to his sidearm, but he didn't draw it. Instead, he gave a soft, humourless laugh. "You think I'm in on this?" he accused Grant, while drumming his fingers on the holster's cover. "You're making a mistake, friend," Dorsey added, his voice cold. "You don't know who you're talking to."

Grant's hand brushed up against the grip of the revolver in his coat pocket. As his eyes locked with Dorsey's, the brief flash of uncertainty that Grant had spotted earlier now gave way to something darker. If he had doubted his instincts earlier, he no longer held a single one. The man was dirty.

"I'm not your friend," Grant replied, his voice steady. "I don't like the way you're dodging these questions. You're hiding something. How long have you been part of this, Dorsey? It's been a while, hasn't it?"

"Careful, Grant. You don't want to start making accusations you can't prove."

Dorsey's gaze shifted. In that moment, Grant saw it: the flicker of guilt that told him everything he needed to know. Before he could press further, Dorsey's hand opened the flap on his holster and drew his Adams revolver.

The world seemed to slow as Grant reacted. As he was drawing the revolver from his coat, the hammer caught against the edge of its pocket, costing him valuable time. He wasn't as fast as Dorsey either.

A first shot rang out, cutting through the air like a clap of thunder. Dorsey's bullet whizzed past Grant's ear, nicking the lobe as it passed. Grant's shot followed a second later and he hit his mark. The bullet struck Dorsey in high in the left shoulder, sending him reeling backward in his saddle.

With a hiss of pain, Dorsey pulled hard on his reins, spurring his horse into motion. Blood was already starting flow freely from the wound, but he didn't stop. He rode hard and fast between Grant and Lillian.

As Grant wheeled about in the saddle and levelled his gun to fire a second shot, Lillian crossed his field of fire. He pulled his revolver up and back, breaking the aim and allowing Dorsey to continue his escape downhill without another shot.

Lillian, already on the move, was urging her horse forward. "Chase him!" she said, her voice urgent.

Grant called after her, "No!" As she turned back towards him wearing a look of disbelief, Grant shook his head, "He's already gone. Let him go."

As Dorsey disappeared down the trail, Grant sat still in his saddle for a moment, before reaching to his ear. The sharp sting of pain and the blood that he saw on his gloves told him how close he had come to being on the losing end of that sudden gun battle.

Despite what Dorsey said, Grant didn't need to prove anything. He now knew Dorsey had been working with McCade. The mole was no longer hidden, but neither was the danger they faced. Grant wondered how deep Dorsey's rot had compromised the Log Cabin. It was only a matter of time before McCade made his move. With Dorsey wounded and retreating, Grant's instincts confirmed that now more than ever, they had to get to White Pass before it was too late.

CHAPTER XVI

No Man's Land

From the western slopes of Turtle Mountain, Grant and Lillian had found an outcropping that allowed them some relative shelter from the elements. The sun had already slipped behind the mountains ahead of them. The sky was free of clouds and the last vestiges of daylight allowed a view out over the wilds and network of small lakes that lead towards the longer, blued finger of Summit Lake.

Beyond that another climb waited, and after that lay White Pass: their destination. They had managed to scrouge up some wood and kindling from the area around their camp. Tonight, they would enjoy the luxury of a small fire. Lillian had even picked off a pair of hares that she had expertly dressed and were now skewered and cooking over the fire.

Fresh meat, another luxury.

Lillian's eyes were sharp. The way she seemed to always have a plan, even when things seemed impossible, both intrigued and unsettled him. He thought about McCade's plan to eliminate all the Mounties at White Pass with sharpshooters. Considering the easy work she had made of the hares at distance, Lillian must have been one of them. Would she have picked off the men with the same ease and detachment? That thought made him shiver.

Grant's mind veered away from their shared vista of the snow-covered peaks and the lonely path ahead. His thoughts were a maelstrom trying to decipher the intersections between the woman riding alongside him; McCade the man who hunted them; and now Dorsey, a traitor to his fellow Mounties.

He could feel Lillian watching him as he thought. It was clear she had something on her mind, something important. She coughed and then announced, "I have a plan."

Glancing at him from the corner of her eye, her tone was calm as she waited for Grant.

"A plan?" he repeated, as he scrutinized her. "What kind of plan?"

Her gaze was steady, as though measuring the weight of her words. "A plan and a confession. I wasn't the only one in the gang who wanted out," she confessed. "We were planning to double cross McCade once we hit White Pass."

"Is that the plan or the confession?" Grant inquired but otherwise held his tongue.

"In the chaos of the attack, we would take off with a few of the pack horses carrying the gold and head back into the Yukon."

"McCade wouldn't chase you?"

"He would think about it, he'd be pissed, but he wouldn't risk heading back after us. Murphy and everyone else wouldn't let him. They'd all want to get across the border and back down to Skag for their payday. We'd leave enough gold to keep everyone greedy."

"How does this help us now?"

"Well, they're still riding with the gang. If I can connect with them somehow, they'll help us. I'm sure of it."

Grant blinked, processing her words. He couldn't tell if this was a legitimate offer of help or some manipulation. "And you trust them?" he asked, and despite his best efforts, his voice was laced with scepticism.

Lillian's lips tightened, and for a moment, Grant saw something flicker in her eyes. It was gone too quickly for him to be sure.

"I trust them enough," She answered. "They want to be quits with McCade: bad. I don't think they'll back out."

Grant followed up with, "Who is it?"

"Riggs," She answered, then added, "But there's more."

Whistling, Grant nodded his head. "Alright, the big guy." He raised an eyebrow and said, "Go on, what else?"

She hesitated, chewing on the inside of her cheek for a moment before speaking again. "The thing is, aside from getting to Riggs, the real plan is risky, but it could be a better option. We don't have to go straight to White Pass and make a stand up there. We lead McCade on a wild goose chase, lure them off the trail. We can thin out their numbers and give ourselves more time for your reinforcements to arrive."

A part of Grant wanted to dismiss her suggestion and stick to the plan he'd made. They would get to White Pass, raise the alarm and then hunker down with the other Mounties to repel McCade's attack. Eliminate the element of surprise and turn it back on the outlaws. He wanted to rely on the law to do its work. However, there was something in her voice, something in her eyes, made it impossible to ignore her.

Waiting for Grant to reply, Lillian added, "I didn't say it was a great plan. Once McCade sees us, he'll want his revenge," she continued, "As far as he's concerned, White Pass can wait until he's killed us."

"Let's say they follow us, then what? How do we thin them out?" Grant asked.

What she proposed next wasn't just a diversion. It was far more dangerous. "We lead them into a trap and take them out." Lillian met his gaze head-on. "Dynamite," she said simply. "It's what I do best."

Grant's stomach dropped at the word. The idea of using explosives was not only reckless, but it was also deadly. The risks were immense. "Where are we going to get dynamite?"

"My saddlebags. I didn't leave that behind, believe me."

"You're serious," he said, shaking his head. "One mistake, one wrong move and it could be our lives we're playing with."

"We're already playing with our lives." She countered. "Listen, I know what I'm doing," her voice was unwavering. "Controlled explosions. We can take them out in one move. When the dust settles, we'll have what we need: McCade and his gang broken. Threat eliminated."

Grant considered her plan. It was audacious, maybe even brilliant in its simplicity. But it didn't sit well with him. Not entirely. She had her own agenda, and Grant wasn't sure where that left him. Was she truly trying to help, or was this just one of her schemes?

"When you're done with the dynamite, then what?" He asked her. "Where does that leave you? With the gold? You and Riggs riding off with McCade's loot?" He couldn't supress the suspicion dripping through his voice.

Lillian's expression tightened, but she didn't flinch. "It's not like that. It leaves me with whatever I decide to do next," she said without emotion. "This isn't about the gold, Grant." She paused, "Not just about the gold. I'm doing this for everyone who's ever suffered under McCade's rule. I mean to end him."

Grant shifted uncomfortably by the fire. "What if I want McCade arrested? Not frontier justice, but justice through the law?" he asked quietly, meeting her eyes.

"That's not in the cards for him." She replied.

"You're asking me to trust you."

Lillian didn't back down. "Yes," she said, her voice was firm. "Because you have no choice. You need me just as much as I need you. This is bigger than your law or my past. If we do something now, we have a chance to save lives. Your bothers in arms, their lives."

"By taking lives."

"Yes," was her simple reply.

For a long moment, neither of them spoke. Grant looked at her, weighing his options. His instincts as a Mountie screamed at him to do things by the book, to follow the rules, to arrest this man. But the reality of the situation was stark. McCade was out there, getting closer by the minute and he wasn't getting any weaker. If Grant and Lillian didn't act now, if they didn't take the risk, they could lose this opportunity to stop him. Could he really trust her? Could he risk his duty, and his life, on her word alone?

"I'll help," he finally said, his voice quiet and resolute. "We'll do it your way. But: no secrets, Lillian. I need to know everything you've got planned."

Lillian nodded, her lips curving into a faint smile, though there was no warmth in it. "Sounds like a fair deal."

The air between them had been heavy with unspoken tension, each carrying their own burden. It was clear that whatever came next, nothing would ever be the same. They had a trap to set, and the stakes were higher than ever.

"Saddle bags full of dynamite, really?" Grant asked with a chuckle.

"A girl's got to keep some secrets." She replied with a laugh of her own. This time, the laugh was open and perhaps honest for the first time since Grant had known her.

"What else have you got it there?"

"Hard tack, jerky." Lillian said. "And, a little whiskey."

"Don't hold back on the feast, break out that bottle!" Grant exclaimed.

With a wide smile, she purred, "I thought you'd never ask."

CHAPTER XVII

The Race to White Pass

The wind whistled down the slopes as McCade's gang climbed the trail above the tree line of twisted spruce towards Turtle Mountain. Leaving the Tutshi Valley behind them, the first sign of the trouble ahead of them arrived. One of the advance scouts fired a shot in the air, followed by a distant shout that echoed down the trail to the rest of the gang, "Rider!"

"Hold up, boys," McCade called out, his voice steady and commanding. He lifted a hand, signalling the men behind him to stop in their tracks.

They waited, their breath forming puffs of vapour in the cold, while the snow crunched underfoot as their horses shifted about beneath them. The scout appeared higher up on the trail, leading a lone rider down to meet them. He was slumped over in the saddle, leaning against the neck of his horse. The animal's legs trembled beneath the burden of its rider, and the bloodstain that had run down its neck. Its rider looked more like a ragged ghost than a man.

"Dorsey," McCade muttered, recognizing the rider.

THE DEADHORSE TRAIL

The man's pale expression was grim, though his eyes held a flicker of recognition when they met McCade's.

"McCade," Constable Dorsey's voice was hoarse, thick with pain. "Didn't think I'd see you this soon." His eyes were drifting and unfocused, yet he noticed McCade's Buffalo Coat, "Nice coat."

"Get him down," McCade ordered.

Two of his men, Milton and Sawyer, moved quickly, one to steady the horse, the other to catch the injured Constable as he collapsed down from his saddle.

The other members of the gang circled around in wait; their expressions wary. None of them questioned McCade's command. He could almost sense the gang's collective thought, *Another Constable?*

The wind picked up again, biting at their exposed skin. Dorsey collapsed heavily onto the ground, gritting his teeth against the pain. Sawyer pulled back Dorsey's own Buffalo Coat to reveal the red serge of the NWMP uniform jacket beneath it. Sawyer showed McCade that it was soaked through with blood, when he pulled his hand back revealing that his fingers were stained red.

"He's been shot," Sawyer confirmed.

"You been in a scrap, Dorsey?" McCade asked with a hint of amusement, as his sharp eyes studied the constable's wound.

"Ambush," Dorsey said, his voice barely above a whisper. "This Grant and some woman. They ambushed me."

McCade's jaw tightened, the name of Constable Grant sparked a flare of anger deep inside him. He had been anticipating trouble ever since Grant's escape with Lillian. McCade had hoped that Grant wouldn't be a serious obstacle, but now, with Dorsey bloodied and half-dead on the ground before him, it was clear that his adversary was making his move.

"Where?" McCade demanded, his gaze never leaving Dorsey's face.

"They're up the trail, a day ahead maybe? They're making for White Pass, to warn the post about you," Dorsey murmured, his voice a hoarse rasp. "Grant. He sent a warning to Bennett Lake too. It's coming, McCade. They'll send reinforcements."

THE RACE TO WHITE PASS

McCade cursed under his breath, his mind whirling with plans, strategies, and contingencies. He had been counting on the element of surprise, but it seemed that Grant was one step ahead. Still, he wasn't about to let this setback slow him down. He needed to stay focused. There was no time for second-guessing.

"You bring me anything?" McCade asked Dorsey.

The Constable reached weakly into his jacket, fumbling with his stiff fingers. With a painful grunt, he pulled out the folded letter, blood smudging its corners. He handed it to McCade with a tired nod.

McCade opened the letter quickly, scanning its contents. It was a map of the Log Cabin, a vital piece of intelligence. The layout, the defences, the guards: it was all here. If McCade could exploit these weaknesses, his attack on the outpost would be swift and decisive.

"Well, well," McCade muttered to himself, his lips curling into a grin. "Looks like you did your job after all, Dorsey."

The gang's leader straightened, handing the letter to Riggs, who immediately began studying it. McCade looked down at the wounded constable, his face hardening.

"Water," Dorsey pleaded.

"Give him some water," McCade ordered. As Sawyer handed Dorsey a water skin, the Constable began to drink greedily.

"Dorsey," McCade continued, "You're gonna have to keep moving."

Dorsey choked on the water, coughed and blinked in confusion. "What?"

"You heard me," McCade growled. "You're gonna keep moving. Head straight for Bennett Lake and make sure those reinforcements don't show. You tell 'em the whole thing's a bust, understand me? Tell 'em that Grant is the menace. He shot you and he's coming to hit them, not the Log Cabin. His message is a distraction."

Dorsey's eyes flickered, but the look in McCade's eyes invited no dissent. The Constable swallowed hard, his face pale beneath the bloodstains. "You want me to ride all the way there... alone?" Dorsey's voice was a mixture of disbelief and desperation.

98

"That's where you were headed before you found us, right? You'll make it," McCade quipped to the Mountie. "If you don't, there's a lot more at stake than just your miserable life. You know what's coming. You know what'll happen if you don't stop them. Now go, you should get moving before the cold finishes you off."

Dorsey seemed to weigh his options for a moment before he finally nodded weakly, too tired to argue.

McCade turned back to his men, his mind already moving ahead with the next set of orders. "Riggs. Clement. You two ride ahead and scout them out," McCade said, his voice cutting through the tension in the air. "And, Clement? If you get a shot, you take it."

Clement, a grizzled man with a reputation for his sharpshooting, gave a short nod, his fingers brushing against his rifle. "Understood," he muttered, his eyes never leaving McCade.

Without another word, Riggs handed the letter back to McCade. Then, he and Clement mounted up and dispersed up the trail with a quiet efficiency.

As the sound of their horses' hooves faded into the distance in pursuit of their quarry McCade stood for a moment, watching his men ride off. He could feel the prospect of what was ahead. With the damning information in Dorsey's letter, the Log Cabin had to fall. The plan would proceed, no matter what. McCade's gaze swept over the rest of his men, settling on each of them with the same sharp command that had gotten them this far.

He glanced down at Dorsey, who was still slumped against the boulder, his breathing shallow but steady. "Don't die on me, Dorsey," McCade muttered before turning his back on the wounded Constable. He didn't have time to deal with casualties. Not now.

"Money. What about my money?" Dorsey asked as he collected himself from off the ground. "I gave you what you wanted."

"Make your way down to Skagway once you're done. Then you'll get paid."

"I've got nothing to get me there." Dorsey protested.

McCade glared at him and then relented. He still needed the man to accomplish a few last things. "Very well." He reached into

Grant's Buffalo Coat and pulled out a small, but heavy sack. "Here's an advance against the rest. Gold dust." He slapped the bag into Dorsey's hand. "You make sure you follow through and stop those Bennett Lake Mounties from riding, you hear me?"

Dorsey nodded in reply and looked down at the bag in his hand.

"I need to hear you say it." McCade's voice was pure venom. "Say it, Dorsey."

"I understand, I'll stop them." Dorsey affirmed.

"Sawyer," McCade growled, "Get him somewhat patched up, enough that he doesn't bleed out on his ride."

The grizzled medic of the gang nodded and set about padding Dorsey's shoulder with a rudimentary dressing.

McCade had no intention of letting a little thing like a warning derail his plan. Even if Dorsey didn't make it, any reinforcements would be too late to catch them. His gang was back on the move and closing in. The Log Cabin, Grant and Lillian couldn't possibly know what was about to hit them.

McCade reached back into his jacket and brought out the Grant's small brass pocket watch. He flipped its lid open and looked at the dial. They still had few more hours of daylight, but they would ride through the night to catch up to his quarry.

He held the watch to his ear and listened to the movement of its gears tick on. It was a good watch, he thought, as he gave its crown a few twists before clicking the lid closed and returning it to the coat's inner pocket. Time to move.

The game was on. The race was on. There would be only one winner. McCade was determined that it would be him.

"The rest of you," McCade shouted out to the gang, "There's no stopping until we find these traitors. Come on boys, let's get to it!"

CHAPTER XVIII

The Hunter Becomes the Hunted

The wilderness of northern British Columbia lay stretched out before Constable Grant, a raw, unforgiving and yet peaceful expanse. Snow-clad peaks loomed behind him. The pale sun had barely crossed the horizon, lighting the passing clouds to lay shadows that slithered like spectres across the rugged terrain. Here, on the western slopes of Turtle Mountain they had decided to lay their trap.

Grant tugged his coat's collar tighter against the cold and glanced over at Lillian, whose steely gaze was fixed on the narrow mountain trail descending toward them. He admired her calm, her expertise. She had, after all, been the creator of this plan. In fact, he never would have made it this far, let alone escaped from McCade's gang without her. Now, laying this ambush they hoped to end the reign of McCade and his outlaw gang in one decisive blow.

"Ready?" Grant asked, his voice steady despite the undercurrents of anxiety that radiated through him.

Lillian's lips twitched into a brief smile, and for a moment, the harsh landscape of her face softened. "As I'll ever be," she replied, her voice quiet and resolute.

She adjusted the strap of the rifle across her shoulders before she attached the last fuses of the dynamite charges they had hidden to her detonator. Her movements were precise and calculated, just like everything she did. He had watched her as they walked the ridgeline planting her charges. Lillian moved with an ease that made it seem effortless, though Grant knew it wasn't. Her every step was deliberate, each movement was planned.

She was a predator stalking her prey and preparing the killing ground for their arrival.

Methodically she had checked each fuse's length again and again, ensuring that the charges would go off in a controlled sequence, one after the other. It had to be perfect. One wrong move and McCade's gang would scatter, and they would be back to square one: on the run, hunted. Facing down an entire gang of ruthless criminals with nowhere to run but across open terrain would the unpleasant and dire consequence of her plan's failure.

Now laying in their concealed vantage point behind a copse of trees, she bit her bottom lip, deep in concentration. After she secured the last of the fuses in place, she reached into her jacket. Removing a small brass blasting cap, she spun the cartridge in her fingers before slotting it home into its rightful place in the detonator.

With a slow exhalation, she set the detonator down and gave it gentle pat, saying, "There we go. Ready."

The two of them had escaped McCade's gang some nights before. Their departure had been quiet, though deadly. Grant regretted the death of Finley, the young man tasked with guarding him. It had been necessary and Lillian, he mused, could have ended the entire caper there had she not chosen to help and make her own escape with him. The reasons for it remained clouded to Grant, but here, together on this mountain he had no cause to doubt her. They had been running, hoping to stay ahead of the cold grasp of death that was promised if McCade had

THE HUNTER BECOMES THE HUNTED

caught up with them. Now, Grant and Lillian were no longer fleeing, they were going on the offensive.

The trail behind them was a jagged, steep climb down the western side of Turtle Mountain. It was a necessary artery and a path that would lead McCade's gang directly through their trap. They had placed dynamite charges at strategic points along the ridge above that section of trail. The resulting blast would bring down the mountainside and crush McCade's gang beneath a showering blanket of rock and debris.

"It's the waiting game now," Grant observed, shifting his rifle and casting his gaze across the barren landscape. "How close do you think they are?"

Lillian's eyes hardened, her mouth tightening as she thought about the men trailing them. "Close, I hope."

"There's that word you love so much."

Lillian gave a short, hard laugh. "Damn you, Grant. Yes, I 'hope' they're close because I'm crap at waiting. Patience was never my strong point."

"What are you worrying about?"

She didn't answer immediately. Instead, she scanned the horizon with sharp, practiced eyes, her mind already working through the myriad possibilities. "Sharpshooters. If Clement's guys spot us, they can easily pick us off."

Grant offered her a half-smile, "We'll make sure they don't get that chance."

The next hours had passed in silence, the only sounds being the whisper of the wind and the occasional call of a distant raven. Grant kept watch, his eyes trained on the pass, where he expected the gang to appear at any moment. Lillian, her rifle close at hand, sat beside him, her gaze sharp as a hawk's.

"I wonder what time it is?" Grant said.

"Daytime, who cares?" Lillian rebutted.

"I'm used to knowing what time it is." Grant answered. "My watch was in my coat."

"Get a new one," Lillian replied.

"It was my father's," Grant added. "Not easy to replace."

"It's still only a watch. Wait," Lillian said and held up her hand. "Shh. Hear that?"

THE DEAD HORSE TRAIL

The quiet began to be broken up at its edges by the distant sound of horses' hooves. They could hear the growing clip clopping echo down towards them from the uneven, rocky trail. The mountain's western trail had enjoyed more sun over the past days and more of the snow had melted away to reveal the stoney path below.

Peering through a small looking glass, Lilian scoured the switchback trails above. Soon, she settled and found the source of the telltale noises. Other travellers had passed back and forth up the trail since they had been watching it, but this time she hissed as she watched the approaching riders.

"It's them," Lillian muttered, her voice low, barely a whisper. "Damn, just scouts. It's not the whole group."

She handed the glass to Grant, who took it and looked up the rocky trail. As he scanned the landscape, looking to find them, Lillian said, "It's Riggs and that's Clement."

Through the trees, he saw two figures emerge, riding slowly, their eyes scanning the landscape for signs of movement. Grant's pulse quickened, but he held steady. The trap was set, but they had to wait a little longer.

Riggs, the muscle of McCade's crew, was no fool. He had a reputation for being cruel and calculating. Lillian had confided that she and Riggs were going to double cross McCade and steal what gold they could. The other man, Grant did not recognize.

"Who's this Clement?" Grant asked as handed back the glass.

"He's a sharpshooter's sharpshooter. About as dangerous a man as I've ever met."

Grant looked at her, sensing her unspoken tension, "You're worried about him."

"Absolutely. Clement's a professional. If he sees us, he'll take the shot and land it."

"What about Riggs? You're still certain he'll help us?"

Riggs and Clement were closing now. They rode through narrow trail's blast area without a care, oblivious to the trap waiting for them further along. They had entered rifle range.

"Lillian?"

"I don't know," she replied. "Yes, I think so."

104

THE HUNTER BECOMES THE HUNTED

"Let's take Clement out," Grant whispered, his voice tight. "It's now or never."

Lillian didn't move. Instead, she leaned forward, eyes narrowed, watching the two men with a mixture of patience and calculation.

"What are you waiting for?" Grant asked, his patience fraying.

She held up a hand, signalling for him to remain quiet.

Grant looked at her, confused.

She met his gaze with an intensity that sent a chill through him. "We wait. Riggs is in on this."

Grant blinked, processing the information. "You're sure?"

"As sure as anyone can be," Lillian's voice was steady, though her eyes betrayed a hint of uncertainty.

Grant's heart pounded in his chest as he took a step back, "Then, Clement?"

Lillian's lips twitched. "He's the one we're waiting for. We'll let them get close. Riggs will help me. He'll give us the moment we need to finish this."

It was a gamble. A dangerous one. But Grant had to trust Lillian's judgment. If anyone could play both sides and come out on top, it was her.

They waited in silence as Riggs and Clement rode towards their position. Clement's eyes flicked over the landscape, his hand resting casually on his rifle. The distance between them was closing, and the tension and anticipation growing unbearable for Grant.

And then, in a split second, Lillian made her move. She fired a shot in the air with her rifle and stood up. She raised the rifle over her head and waved at the two men.

Clement, heard the shot and with practiced ease, swung his rifle towards the sound. Seeing Lillian standing in the open, he exhaled slowly as he took aim. He steadied himself. His finger tightened around the trigger.

A shot rang out. It wasn't a rifle's but rather the sharp crack of a revolver that split the had air. It hadn't been aimed at Grant or Lillian. It had been aimed at Clement.

Clement's body jerked violently. His finger twitched against the trigger of his rifle, and the shot went wide, crashing into the

105

trunk of a tree a few feet to Lillian's left. When the rifle fell from his hands, the sharpshooter sagged back in his saddle, his eyes wide in shock.

Riggs was stopped beside him, the smoking barrel of his revolver aimed squarely at Clement's chest. "You should've known better, Clement," Riggs growled. "You were never part of this plan."

He pulled the trigger again, and the second shot caught Clement centre mass, sending him out the saddle to hit the ground in a heap.

Lillian looked at Grant, her eyes gleaming with a dangerous fire. "The hunter becomes the hunted," she murmured.

For just a moment, Grant allowed himself a small flicker of renewed hope. They might just survive this. The immediate danger had passed, but the weight of what had just transpired hung heavy in the air. Leaving the relative protection of their hiding spot, Lillian and Grant approached Riggs.

The big man stood over Clement's body, his eyes cold, his expression unreadable. Lillian took a cautious step forward and slung her rifle over her shoulder. Her face impassive as she regarded Riggs. She raised her hands, slow and steady to show open hands and no weapons.

Riggs spat on the snow by the crimson stain spreading out around Clement's motionless body. It's bright colour stark against the white landscape. He wiped his hands on his coat, as though erasing any trace of involvement in the bloody moment.

"Didn't think you'd pull it off, Lillian," Riggs muttered, glancing down at Clement's lifeless form. "I thought you'd end up dead in a ditch somewhere. Guess you've got more tricks up your sleeve than McCade thought."

Lillian shrugged, her gaze flicking between Riggs and the distant mountain pass. "I'm full of surprises."

Riggs seemed to take a long, measured look at her, sizing her up in a way that made Grant uncomfortable. For a moment, he wondered if the man was second-guessing his choice to trust her.

"Are we trusting each other?" Riggs's tone was more curious than confrontational.

THE HUNTER BECOMES THE HUNTED

Lillian arched an eyebrow, "You think I'm gonna turn on you now?"

He gave a small, humourless laugh. "Not if you know what's good for you."

The two of them laughed and then hugged each other. It dispelled the remaining tension and uncertainty that hovered around the scene of the kill. Their embrace was tight, warm and genuine but Grant noted there was nothing romantic about it.

When they broke their embrace, Riggs turned to look over at Constable Grant. Lillian followed his gaze, then, with deliberate ease, walked over to Grant and motioned for Riggs to join her. She nodded toward Grant. "You two are gonna have to get reacquainted," Lillian said, her voice flat.

Riggs hesitated, as if deciding if he wanted to be pleasant. "You sure he ain't gone just shoot me?"

"He won't," Lillian cut him off. "I've got him covered."

Riggs's gaze flicked back to the mountainside; his eyes sharp. "If you say so."

With a grunt, Riggs walked over to Grant, who stepped forward, his face unreadable. Lillian followed, standing beside the Constable, her posture stiff, her body language tense as the inevitable moment approached.

"Grant," she said, her voice betraying none of the anxiety that must have been churned beneath her calm exterior. "This is Riggs."

Riggs gave a slight nod, his hand resting on the grip of his revolver, a silent warning to Grant. But Lillian saw the flicker of something else in his eyes, something that hinted at a bond forged out of necessity, not trust.

Grant didn't offer a handshake, but his eyes locked with Riggs' in a way that said he was sizing him up just as much as the big man was sizing the Constable up.

"Didn't expect you to be here," Grant said, his voice was direct and their words weighed heavily between them.

Riggs gave a curt nod, his lips twisted into a half-smile that never quite reached his eyes. "Likewise. Seems we have a common interest, eh?"

Lillian stepped closer, breaking the tension with a soft chuckle. "Under different circumstances, I think you'd have shot him on sight, Riggs."

Riggs didn't flinch at her remark. "Maybe. The lady's got a way of convincing people to change their minds, Grant." His gaze lingered on her for a moment, a strange mix of admiration and wariness in his eyes. "She owes me now. For this little favour; and for Dawson."

Lillian's lips curled slightly, the ghost of a smirk playing across her features. "Oh no, this makes us even," she said. "Just even."

Grant eyed both of them, and asked, "What exactly did you do for her in Dawson, Riggs?"

Riggs chuckled darkly, though it didn't carry much humour. "It's not something you're gonna want to hear, Constable. But if we make it past tomorrow, I might tell you. For now, I'm on your side."

Grant exchanged a glance with Lillian, silently assessing her reaction. He wasn't entirely sure what to make of this new alliance, but he knew they didn't have time to waste. "We work together," he said slowly, keeping his hand near his holster. "For now."

Riggs gave a half-shrug. "As long as we get McCade out of the picture. He's got no loyalty. Not to me, not to anyone. He'll toss us all aside the moment he gets the chance." He paused, eyes flicking towards Lillian, "McCade's not going to take kindly to losing a man like Clement. How are you planning to finish him off?"

Lillian nodded, her expression hardening as she spoke. "We're going to make sure McCade gets a one-way ticket to whatever hell he deserves. Same plan as before, just a little different."

Riggs's eyes narrowed slightly as he looked at Lillian, the flicker of recognition passing between them. "You ever think you're playing too close to the fire, Lillian?" he asked, a quiet challenge in his voice.

She didn't hesitate. "Keeps me warm in the winter."

Grant shifted on his feet, glancing back at the trail, "When McCade comes through here, we'll be ready. How far back are they Riggs?"

THE HUNTER BECOMES THE HUNTED

"Less than a day. Could be a few hours." Riggs' eyes were sharp with purpose. "Let's just hope that it's sooner rather than later."

"Because this one's not good with waiting?" Grant nodded towards Lillian.

Riggs laughed, "Patience is not one of her virtues."

Lillian punched the bigger man in the arm, "You two worry less about my virtues and more about what's next."

The three of them stood there for a moment, the cold mountain air pressing in from all sides. Each of them knew that the game had changed, but none of them knew what the end would look like. One thing was certain: they were in this together now, whether they liked it or not.

CHAPTER XIX

A Message Ignored

Jorge's mount, a strong chestnut mare with a smooth coat trotted steadily along the snow-crusted path. The rider adjusted his grip on the reins, his calloused hands numb from the biting cold. His second horse, carrying his packs, tools and supplies followed behind with the ease of long practice. As they descended towards the rudimentary tented encampment that was spread along the shores of Bennett Lake, Jorge could hear the distant echoes of wolves calling from some hidden corner of the wilderness behind him. Above, the sky was clear, and the morning's sun shone down, warming his face.

It had been days since he had crossed the White Pass, and more recently crossed paths with a Police Constable in need of his help. Since then, he had made his journey without a rest through the frigid northern wilds to deliver the Constable's message. The air was thin here, the snow deep, and the tracks left by his horses were often covered within minutes by the sweeping gusts of wind.

Jorge had no illusions about the challenges of the life he had chosen to lead up to this point. He had ridden alone across vast stretches of the continent. From the barren deserts of Mexico, through America, over the harsh peaks of the Rockies and Coastal Mountains and now, he was approaching the frozen expanse of the Klondike. He'd learned long ago not to care about the discomfort he faced. Today, his duty was clear. He had a purpose.

The message Constable Grant had entrusted to him was simple enough, yet fraught with urgency, *'Send reinforcements to White Pass. The Outpost will soon be under attack by a gang of outlaws. They plan to escape to Alaska. They are well-armed and well-organized. The situation is dire. I am on my way to warn the Outpost there of this imminent threat. Constable Stephen Grant, North-West Mounted Police (Fort Selkirk/Tagish Detachment).'*

As Jorge rode, the weight of the message's warning pressed heavy on his mind. He was struck by the forthright demeanour of the young Constable. He felt that perhaps this was the reason why he found himself here. By helping this young man, he would save some lives in the process. Could any man ask for more of a purpose?

As he descended into the valley, the mountain landscape's monochrome of whites and grey had begun to be broken up by the additions of the greens and sharp outlines of spruce trees. Every few miles, Jorge would glance back over his shoulder, making sure the distant horizon behind him remained clear. It was always the same: empty and silent. Seeing the broad blues of Bennett Lake stretching out ahead, he smiled. He was close to fulfilling his promise.

When he rode through the gates of the NWMP Post later that morning, his arrival was greeted by the cold stare of Sergeant Flynn, the man in charge.

"Rough ride?" Flynn asked, taking the reins of his horse as Jorge dismounted with a grunt of relief.

Jorge nodded, rubbing his frozen fingers together, the feeling slow to return. He said, "Cold as death out there, Sergeant. I have an urgent message for you. It's from Constable Grant."

"Never heard of him," The Sergeant replied.

Removing the scrap of paper from his jacket, Jorge offered it to the man.

A MESSAGE IGNORED

Flynn's brow furrowed as he stepped closer, snapping the page into his hand with a brisk motion. His eyes flicked over the contents, and his expression hardened.

"Damn," Flynn muttered under his breath. He folded the paper, tucking it into the inner pocket of his coat. "We've had word of outlaws operating in the region. There was a gold heist up in Dawson. You're sure this man was a Constable?"

"Si, he was wearing the red jacket. A Mountie, like you."

"This makes it official," his gaze flicked to Jorge, studying him carefully. He said, "You look like you've been riding for days. What's your name?"

"Jorge, Sergeant. Mucho gusto. You will help this Grant?"

"Take yourself some rest Jorge. I'll investigate what we can send for reinforcements," Flynn waved Jorge toward the small cabin that served as both barracks and station house. "Get inside and get some warmth in you."

Jorge was about to reply when the sound of hooves reached his ears. A rider was coming in, fast, the thundering of hooves cutting through the cold air. He turned instinctively, squinting against the sun as the rider grew closer.

It was a man, riding hard, the horse's hooves throwing up clouds of snow. Jorge felt tension fill in the air. It was a Constable, hunched over in the saddle, pale as death, his hands pressed to the reins with grim determination.

He cried out, "Sergeant!"

"Dorsey!" Flynn answered, stepping forward as the constable pulled his blood-stained horse to a stop with a jarring halt.

Dorsey's face was contorted with pain. His eyes were wide, the pupils dilated from the effort of staying conscious. His shoulders sagged as he dismounted. Barely managing to keep his balance, he dropped heavily onto one knee. Blood had soaked through his coat where his shoulder was bound up with makeshift bandages, and his breath came in short, ragged bursts.

"Sergeant," his hoarse voice raped. "We've got trouble."

Flynn crouched beside him in an instant, his face hardening as he saw the blood staining Dorsey's uniform. "I've got you man. What happened? Who did this to you?"

Dorsey shook his head slowly, wincing from the movement. "It was Grant," he murmured, his voice barely more than a whisper.

Jorge froze. The mention of Grant's name sent an icy shiver down his spine.

Flynn did not conceal his confusion. He asked, "Grant? The gang making for White Pass? Yes, I've just heard about it."

Dorsey swallowed hard, his breath coming in short gasps. He looked up at Flynn, his gaze filled with a mix of disbelief and fear. "No," he said. "Grant's the one leading them. The outlaws. He's not heading to White Pass. He's coming here, to hit you. It's all a trap."

Jorge took a step forward, his mind racing. The words hung in the air, sharp and chilling.

"What do you mean?" Flynn asked, his tone turning colder, more urgent. "Are you saying Grant is with the outlaws?"

Dorsey nodded grimly, his face pale and drawn. "He's the one who led them through our camp. They already took the Log Cabin. I barely got out of there alive. He's on his way here now, he's going to attack this post."

"This man brought me a message from Grant." Flynn told Dorsey. "He says the gang is going to attack the Log Cabin."

"No, he already has. I'm telling you! That's a diversion to lead you away from here."

Jorge's heart pounded in his chest. This was impossible. It didn't make sense.

Dorsey gripped Flynn's arm, his fingers trembling, and whispered, "You don't understand. I saw him. He's leading them. He killed our men before we even knew what was happening. I tried to stop him. They're coming for you next, Sergeant. His gang's coming for you." The weight of exhaustion overtook him and he passed out without further news.

"Dorsey? Dorsey!" Flynn shook him, but the Quartermaster remained unconscious. "Get the Doctor here sharpish!" he barked to the other Constables who had arrived and heard the end of Dorsey's speech. He then added, "Get this man inside."

"Grant is no traitor," Jorge old Flynn in a hushed tone. "I only met him as he was making the climb, not two days ago. He had not reached the pass. I had crossed a few days before that. There was no attack."

"I don't know this Grant, but I know this man. He's a trusted member of the detachment. I have no reason to doubt him," Flynn shot back. His jaw tightened as he slowly straightened up, casting a glance toward Jorge, then back at Dorsey.

The silence in the air grew heavy, the wind howling through the trees, flapping the canvas of the tents nearby like a distant warning.

As the Constables carried Dorsey's limp body into the barracks, Jorge's heart was heavy with disbelief. He looked at Flynn. "What will you do now?"

The Sergeant's gaze was dark and unreadable. "I'm not sending any reinforcements, for one thing," he said with resolve. "We'll hold our ground."

The cold and fatigue bore down on his shoulders with crushing force. Jorge hesitated for only a moment, and when he spoke, he felt his heart race. "I'll go back to White Pass. I'll find out the truth and then return. You need to know what is happening up there."

Flynn's eyes sharpened, "Why would you go?"

"For the same reason I agreed to carry Grant's message. It is the right thing to do," was his earnest reply. "I've ridden this far, Sergeant. If Grant has lied to me, used me, then I must know. If he is planning an attack, I will see him and this gang coming. I can be back here before him and warn you."

"How do I know you're not in on it?" Flynn challenged Jorge. "I should detain you until I know more."

"You can do that, but then you may never know. No, I must know the truth of this. I will leave you my other horse, Esmerelda. She carries all of my outfit. All my possessions. She has made the ride all the way with me from Mexico. I will be back for her. I care more for her than what she carries."

Flynn's lips pressed into a thin line. He muttered, "God help you, Jorge."

With that sentiment, which Jorge hoped was more a blessing than a curse, he swung back onto his horse. His heart pounded in his chest. "If I get to White Pass and all is as Grant said, then that Constable is not who you think he is."

THE DEAD HORSE TRAIL

"He's not going anywhere in his condition," Flynn remarked, then nodded his head. "I hear what you're saying Jorge, I'll keep him here until you return."

"Then I shall see you and Esmerelda again soon." Jorge replied and he urged his horse into motion.

The path ahead was uncertain, and with every step, it grew darker for Jorge.

"I will know the truth of this," he whispered to himself as he rode west. The horse's hooves struck the snow as Jorge kicked it into a gallop, racing into the wind and snow, back the way he had come. He couldn't shake the growing feeling that he was riding towards a storm.

CHAPTER XX

Ambush!

Riggs had hoped for McCade and the gang to arrive sooner rather than later. His hope soon became a reality and Lillian's patience was spared a long wait. The cold bite of the Klondike morning nipped at Grant's skin. The trail before the gang, a jagged scar winding its way down the mountainside was narrow and treacherous.

    Beside Grant, Lillian and Riggs were crouched low, their eyes fixed on the winding path that led towards their hide in the trees. It was planned as the perfect ambush, if only they could get it right. The moment the first explosion rang out, chaos would follow. They had to trust their plan, no matter how risky it was.

    A few hundred yards away, McCade and his gang were moving, their shadows casting out before them in the morning's sunlight. As they made their way downhill, they remained unaware of the trap. Grant could see McCade at the front, his hat tipped low against the wind. His movements were fluid, nothing like the blundering outlaws that Grant had encountered before this.

    "Bastard's wearing my coat," Grant observed as his hand tightened around his Winchester Repeater. He flicked a glance at

Lillian. She gave a brief nod, her eyes focused, hard with purpose. She had been a member of McCade's gang once. It may have felt like a lifetime ago that she had been one of them, riding rough and free, but it had only been mere days that she had quit the gang. Regardless, Grant thought she was a far different woman today. A woman with a deadly purpose.

Next to her, Riggs wore a grim smile under his frost lined beard. It pulled at the corners of his mouth as he watched the approaching gang. Like Lillian, he was another defector from the gang, though this alliance was only a few hours old. Despite the cold, his hands were steady as they waited for their moment.

"Do it," he growled at Lillian.

With a quick twist of the detonator's handle, she set their plan in motion. Grant heard a loud pop as the blasting cap fired, setting off the fuses. The lines ignited with a hiss and sped away from their hide, giving off small puffs of white putrid smoke as they burnt.

"How long?" Grant whispered, his voice low.

"Not long," Riggs replied in his low gravelled voice. It was the unmistakable rare sound of an old outlaw, "When you hear the boom, their goose is cooked."

Grant glanced up towards the ridge where they'd planted the dynamite. Carefully hidden above the descending gang, the charges waited for their moment. The mountainside had swallowed up their preparations whole, and now, all they had to do was wait for the fuses to reach those hidden bundles. It was the burning fuses that he worried about now. He could see the small puffs of smoke rising from the ground as they burnt their way up the side of Turtle Mountain.

"They're going to see that," Grant said, giving voice to his worries.

"Even if they do it's too late now," Lillian shot back.

McCade pulled back on the reins of his horse, pausing to light a cigar. He waved others past him as he puffed away, encouraging the match's flame at its foot to burn. Grant held his breath as he watched McCade toss away the match and exhale a huge cloud of smoke into the air.

AMBUSH!

Then, there it was: a low rumble, barely perceptible at first, but a loud crack broke through the silence. The ground trembled beneath their feet before the world exploded upward.

The series of blasts made a deafening series of roars as the dynamite's guttural booms rippled along and punctured the air. The path in front of the gang disappeared into a dirty white fog. Snow and rocks erupted into the air. The massive cloud of smoke and dust engulfed the trail, obscuring everything from view in mere seconds. The trees shook, quivering as if they protested the sudden violence. Snow, rock, and debris tumbled down the mountainside in a torrent.

Grant's heart raced as he looked at the haze, waiting for a sign of the gang. McCade? There was nothing. He couldn't make out anyone. As the dust began to settle and be blown away by the winds, then he saw it: movement.

McCade's gang wasn't gone. They hadn't been obliterated in the blast. As the smoke cleared further, Grant's stomach dropped. Their timing had been off.

The outlaws had been spread out as they descended the trail. The time it had taken for the fuses to burn their way to the charges had allowed the gang clear much of the blast area, avoiding the worst of it. Some of the gang had been hit square on, while others had been knocked from their horses. The lead element of the gang appeared to still be mounted.

McCade was wheeling about on his horse, trying to control it while looking for the cause of the blast and their attackers. The blast had however separated the vanguard of the gang from their train of pack horses at their rear. Those horses carried the precious cargo of the stolen gold. An enormous debris field now lay between the gang and their prize.

"Damn it," Lillian muttered, her face a mask of frustration.

Riggs didn't waste time, "We can't wait here. We need to move."

The sound of shouting reached their ears. Grant watched as McCade fought to calm his horse while yelling at the gang to regroup and figure out what had happened.

Grant's fingers twitched, ready for the fight. Riggs was right, they had to take advantage of the chaos. The three of them had to move fast, or they would be surrounded. For a fleeting moment, the hunter had become the hunted, but that moment had passed. They had missed their shot and would soon become the hunted once again.

"Move!" Grant shouted and sprinted for their horses. As he slung his rifle over his shoulder, Lillian and Riggs were close behind him.

After the first explosion rattled across the mountainside, McCade had been thrown off his horse. The force of the successive blasts had also knocked his horse to the ground. He grunted in pain and scrambled to his feet. His ears were ringing as the blasts continued one after the next.

Ambush! The realization hit him like a cold slap. The air was thick with the acrid scent of smoke and snow, and through the haze he saw his men were scattered, confusion clouding their faces.

In a swift motion he swung himself back into the saddle while his horse regained its footing. The animal was terrified and McCade hung on for dear life as he tried to calm his spooked mount and not be thrown again. It took all his strength to stay on the beast's back as it spun about in terror. It was through force of will, extreme bad language and sheer determination that brought the horse back under his control.

As the smoke from the blast cleared, McCade didn't waste a second. His mind snapped into focus, cutting through the chaos as his eyes darted over the scene. His men were scrambling about, disoriented. Some lay dead in the snow by their downed horses.

"Get up!" McCade bellowed, his hoarse voice commanding the living. "Move! Get to cover!"

He looked out across the landscape. Where was the threat? From behind a small cluster of trees below their position, he saw three horses ride hard for the trail leading towards the lakes and mountains to the west.

Above those mountains the sky was darkening, filling with the angry clouds of a stormfront hurtling towards them from across White Pass.

"Lillian. Grant. And Riggs? You too? Turncoat," he spat out the word through clenched teeth.

His frustration only grew when he turned back to look up the trail. The dynamite had done more damage than he had expected. Lillian's handiwork. She had been his ace-in-the-hole for the assault on White Pass. He surveyed the snow, the rocks and the bodies of his men. The trail had been destroyed and now boulders and heaps of shattered, impassable rubble lay between him and the gold. They had spread the heavy loads across their train of packhorses. Those startled animals were panicked and in disarray, scattering as they climbed back up the mountain with their precious heavy cargoes in tow. The two men of his rearguard was doing the best to regain control of the train, animal by animal.

The gold, the treasure that he and his men had fought for, died for and struggled to bring this far? They were cut off from their spoils. The loot they had rightfully stolen had been stolen from them. Grant. Grant had become more than a thorn in McCade's paw. He was a parasite. One that needed to be rooted out and destroyed. McCade cursed Grant's name and cursed himself for not seeing the trap. His eyes burned with a thirst for bloody revenge. He could no longer have his prize and now the only reward that mattered to him was vengeance. A cold comfort.

"You think you've taking me down with this Grant? Not happening," he said before turning to his remaining men. He shouted, "Get your damn rifles! They're running! I will see them dead before I let them walk away from this!"

As the swirling winds of the approaching storm reached them, McCade ignored it. His mind was boiling over with hate. His eyes swept over his men, still slow to regain their bearings. They were scared, shaken, but McCade wasn't having any of it. He stepped his horse forward and slid his rifle from the sheath hanging off his saddle. With a sneer, he bellowed, "Don't you dare let that dynamite get in your head. We're hunters. They are prey! They might've caught us off guard, but now the game's on."

He raised his rifle, pointing toward the mountains and the storm. "We move! We keep moving and by the time they realize we're on them; it'll be too late."

THE DEAD HORSE TRAIL

A few of his men hesitated, but McCade's gaze bore into them, sharp and fierce. "You wanted to take the Log Cabin? That's where they're headed. Our gold? It's gone! All we can get is what we take from the Mounties at White Pass. Plus the pound of flesh I'm gonna cut out of Grant, Lillian and Riggs. Revenge, that's it! They stole the gold from you. We're going after them. They're not getting away with this. Now MOVE!"

McCade's words cut through the confusion, the men rallied with this new focus. They weren't completely unscathed, but they were determined and now they were angry. They had lost their payday. With McCade at the helm, they knew there was still a chance to turn the tide.

"Let's finish this," McCade snarled and with that, the gang moved forward. They had become a relentless force that was eager for revenge.

CHAPTER XXI

The Chase

As their horses climbed away from the valley and lakes towards White Pass, Lillian, Riggs and Grant had been enveloped by the oncoming storm's furious embrace. Grant was unsure of what the future held for them though he knew this phase of the fight was far from over. McCade wasn't the type to let a trap be the end of him. He would keep coming. With their gold lost, Grant knew the gang wouldn't stop until McCade had his prize: their heads.

The snowstorm howled around them as the three of them rode up towards White Pass. The trail had narrowed, the rocks and snow on either side forming jagged cliffs that seemed to close in from above. The world around them was a blur of snow and stone, a maelstrom of white. Grant's breath came in sharp bursts. He forced himself to focus, trying not to let the adrenaline cloud his thoughts. The heavy breathing of the horses behind him signalled that Lillian and Riggs were still with him. There was no time to look back. McCade's gang was relentless.

"Not much farther now," Grant called out to them. The storm was clearing slightly, but the trail ahead remained treacherous.

His eyes were scanning ahead, his lips pressed into a thin line. "I can see a ridge ahead."

Riggs caught up to Grant, his face stern. "McCade knows these mountains. The whole damn gang is going to be on us like wolves on a hunt."

Grant pointed up ahead saying, "We make it to the ridge, then pick them off as they climb. They've got no other route to get by us. It'll give us a fighting chance. If we're lucky, we can slow them down while they regroup."

Lillian nodded. "Lucky doesn't last long in these parts," she muttered.

Grant knew she was right. But they didn't have the luxury of choice. This was the right spot to make a stand. The path up to the ridge was steep and the snow was thickening. Grant could hear the distant rumble of the storm shifting once again. As the wind picked up with a sudden intensity, it howled through the pass like an angry animal.

From where they tied up their horses, Riggs led the way down to the ridgeline. His movements were quick and sure, though he too was fighting against the elements. His coat was frayed at the edges and threadbare. It must have offered little warmth, though there was no slowing him down. He was driven, and that could make the difference between life and death in these mountains.

Lillian moved into position beside Grant, her face tight with concentration. "We won't hold them for long," she observed quietly, "We don't have the ammo to make some last stand."

Grant didn't look at her. His eyes stayed fixed on the ridge ahead. He said, "I know. We push them back and then we make for the Log Cabin. Thin the herd again. That's the best we can do."

Lillian glanced back at the trail behind them. She seemed to be looking for something more than just the looming threat of McCade's men. Maybe she was hoping for the impossible, the moment where they'd make it out of this alive. Grant didn't blame her.

The mountains loomed above the ridge as the wind swirled between their grey walls, making it difficult to see. Riggs motioned to a cluster of rocks up ahead, "Here. It'll give us some cover from anyone coming up from below."

THE CHASE

Lillian agreed, "It's a good spot."

"Let's get set up," Grant ordered, his voice sharp. "We'll make this quick."

Riggs and Lillian moved to the rocks, taking positions to fire from hidden angles. Snowflakes stung their faces as they settled into this new ambush. As they waited, the cold seeped into their bones. The wind howled louder, the storm continuing to shift as it tore its way across the mountains. All three of them knew what was coming.

"Ready?" Grant asked them, his voice steady despite the chaos raging in his head.

Lillian gave him a single nod, her eyes sharp as she checked her rifle one last time. "Let's hope this works," Riggs muttered under his breath. He pulled out the battered stub of a cigar from his coat and proceeded to light it with a match. Despite the wind, it was done with expert flair. He puffed out a cloud of smoke and said, "McCade won't split up the gang. They'll push through. We'll take out the first wave, then we deal with whoever's left."

"Where did that stogey come from?" Lillian asked.

"Kept it for a special occasion," he replied. "Also kept me one of these." He pulled a single stick of dynamite from the jacket and waved it around with a smirk. "Always good to have a party favour."

"Did you steal that off me?" Lillian countered.

"Ages ago," he replied, then stuffed it back into an inside pocket of his coat.

"Thief," Lillian observed.

"Guilty as charged. Perhaps the Constable should take me into custody?" Riggs offered.

As Grant, Lillian, and Riggs crouched low behind the rocks, their bodies grew stiff with the cold and anticipation. The storm's steady flurries of snow swirled in gusts that made everything around them seem to vanish into the white void. The mountains felt alive, a vast wilderness that had witnessed countless struggles for survival.

The Winchester felt heavy in Grant's hands, but it was a comfort. It was the only thing between him and the gang that was closing in. Watching for any sign of movement, Grant's eyes scanned the snowy expanse below. Despite the storm, there was an eerie quiet, the kind that always preceded danger.

As the minutes that felt like hours passed, he glanced toward Riggs, who began to peer through a small gap between the rocks. His eyes narrowed as he scanned the trail. "They're coming," Riggs murmured. "I can see them. Just below us. There: the edge of the pass."

Grant's heart skipped. The first of McCade's men appeared in the distance, their forms barely visible through the snow, but their silhouettes were unmistakable against the white backdrop. Two riders were climbing fast with another three right behind them. Each held their rifle up and ready, their breath swirling in the cold. The men were pushing hard, confident in their horses.

Holding his breath, Grant waited, counting the seconds. The wind tore at his face, the snow stung his eyes, but he kept the rifle steady. "Hold," he said, his voice barely audible over the wind.

Lillian and Riggs both nodded, already set in their positions. Grant exhaled a long, slow breath, adjusted his grip on the rifle and lined up his shot.

He could feel the storm closing in around them, the chaos coming fast from below. His muscles tightened; his senses sharpened. For a moment, everything fell into a perfect stillness. It was the calm before the storm.

"Now!" Grant shouted, and in an instant, gunfire erupted. Their rifles' sharp reports echoed down the ravine chasing their bullet's paths that had already found their homes inside flesh. The first two men were down, dropped by Grant and Lillian. Riggs had fired two shots and felled both lead horses. The tangled debris created by those bodies was crashed into by the riders close behind.

The impact threw those men over the necks of their horses and into the snow. The first wave of the gang was in sudden disarray. As the riders below tried to recover from the sudden chaos, rounds continued to be fired down at them from the ridge. Grant aimed at the shadows of the outlaws as they scrambled for cover. Lillian was doing the same, while Riggs continued to shoot the horses. It was calculated and in Grant's mind cruel, but the circumstances required a determined lack of conscience.

THE CHASE

The snow made it hard to see and Grant felt the rush of danger. It was like a river's strong current, pulling him deeper into the fight.

Having taken cover behind their dead horses, the gang now began to return fire. The snap of their bullets mingled with the wind and the pounding of approaching hooves further down the ravine. Grant ducked as a bullet whizzed past, narrowly missing him. He returned fire, but the gang was already regrouping. Grant scrambled further along the ridgeline, ducking behind the rocks, his heart racing. His breath came in shallow, quick bursts as he kept his eyes on the position of the gang below.

They held the high ground. They had this moment, a small window to inflict some more damage on the gang. He kept low, moving silently across the rocky ledge, trying to stay hidden in the snow flurries. His muscles screamed with the effort, his limbs trembling from the cold, but he didn't stop.

He stopped, knelt by a large boulder and aimed his rifle downhill. He exhaled slowly then squeezed the trigger. His shot rang out, sharp and loud, echoes bouncing off the rock walls.

The bullet hit its mark: a man at the edge of the group fell to the snow with a grunt, clutching his chest. Grant crouched behind the boulder's cover, pressing his back against its cold rock. His fingers were stiff with the cold, but he gripped his rifle tightly. He needed to get to a better vantage point. The gang wasn't far off now, he could hear their gathering shouts below. They would chase and continue to chase until they had their revenge.

To his left, Grant could hear Riggs and Lillian firing back, their aim steady and shots selective. Lillian was racking rounds into the chamber of her rifle and dispatching them with the calm precision of someone who had fought beside McCade before.

They were outnumbered, but the terrain and conditions were working in their favour. Grant peeked out to get another look at the gang's position. He remained confident that they could disorganize and slow the gang down enough to get some distance between them.

Another shot rang out, the bullet ricocheting off the stone and snow just inches from his head. Grant ducked back. The rush of wind as it passed was too close for comfort. McCade's men had begun moving uphill using the cover of the rocks. Intent on closing the gap to their attackers, they covered each other with a practiced efficiency.

"Riggs, to your right!" Grant barked as he moved along the ridge, dodging another spray of gunfire.

Riggs reacted immediately, his broad frame moving expertly as he turned, fired and took cover. Lillian followed Riggs, sliding to the left, cutting across the narrow trail to keep their attackers off balance. The sound of gunfire echoed around them, a constant barrage as McCade's men kept their distance but were making a steady advance.

"Get to the horses!" Grant instructed Riggs, then covered the big man as he ran uphill for the horses. He emptied his rifle and took cover to reload. While he slammed fresh rifle cartridges into the receiver of the Winchester, Lillian stood up to shoot.

Another round of shots rang out, and this time, the sound was accompanied by the sickening thud of a bullet hitting flesh. Lillian's cry tore through the air, and Grant whipped around. He saw her stagger for a moment, then she went down hard, her knees buckling beneath her. Still holding her rifle in one hand, her left was clutched to her chest just below the collar bone of her right shoulder.

"Lillian!" Grant called out, his voice a mix of fear and anger. Without hesitation, he ran towards her and helped her stand, "Can you move?" his voice was tight, desperation had crept in.

Lillian, winced with pain, gritting her teeth. "Leave me, damn it. I'll cover you!"

Grant shot a glance back downhill towards the gang. McCade was leading the charge now, despite the murk, his figure was unmistakable in the chaos. Grant could hear him urging his men further up the slope. He didn't care about the gold anymore; this was personal. Leaving her behind was a death sentence.

"Not a chance, let's go. Move your legs!" Grant insisted and began to drag her towards Riggs and the horses. The snow crunched beneath their boots as they scrambled up the slope. As they climbed, the gunfire stopped.

THE CHASE

A voice, McCade's voice, boomed out through the snowstorm. "You can't run forever, Grant! We'll get you!"

"Come on!" Riggs yelled as he swung himself up into the saddle. He levelled his rifle and emptied its remaining shots down the hill at two men trying to take the ridgeline just behind Grant and Lillian. The first shot missed, but the second hit its mark, striking one of McCade's men in the shoulder. The outlaw went down tumbling backwards over the ridge. The last two bullets ended the second man, who crumped into a heap in the snow.

Riggs threw the now empty rifle into the snow and kicked his horse over towards Grant. He cried out, "Give her to me!"

The animalistic intensity of McCade's furious voice called out to them again, "You think you've won, Grant? You're just buying time, and that's all it is. Time."

Without any effort Riggs snatched Lillian up from Grant's arms and her draped her over his lap like a ragdoll.

"Now move, Copper!" he barked. He drew the single stick of dynamite from his coat and held its fuse against the smouldering stub of his cigar. When the fuse caught and sputtered to life, he said, "Party time."

Riggs threw the stick downhill before he turned his horse and savagely raked his spurs across its ribs, pressing it to climb.

Grant watched the dynamite sail over the ridge and disappear into the white void. He cursed under his breath, then hauled himself up into his saddle. The whirling snow was covering their escape as they rode up the narrow trail toward White Pass. The sound of the gang's gunfire renewed and echoed behind him, a steady rhythm of revenge.

A dull thud behind them told Grant that the last stick of dynamite had detonated, but without any noticeable effect, the gunshots continued to ring out behind them and bullets snapped past their heads. One bullet grazed his coat. It felt it snatch at the material by his arm like a phantom's touch.

The voice of McCade sliced through the wind again, "There they are!"

Grant's heart lurched in his chest. He feared it would only be a moment or two now before a bullet tore into his back, ending all

THE DEAD HORSE TRAIL

of his plans. He leant low against his horse and willed it to ride faster. A loud crack split the air.

The world below seemed to explode below them. The snow around, and behind them became a seething tide of white, as it spilled down from the slopes. Grant inhaled with sharp terror. Avalanche!

It roared down the mountain slopes like a living thing, sweeping away everything in its path. It poured across the ridge and filled the air with a thick fog of ice and powder. The rumble of the avalanche was deafening.

Grant urged his horse forward, his pulse quickening. "Ride hard!" but his shout was drowned out by the avalanche.

Riggs needed no encouragement to keep climbing. The big man was screaming into the winds as they climbed and climbed.

They were away and out of the avalanche's path. The gunfire had stopped and the path ahead of them had widened, revealing the trail led to a series of narrow switchbacks carving their way higher along the rockface. At speed, it was a risky route. One fall would spell a fatal end to the chase. It was their only way forward.

Riggs, with Lillian laid across his lap, pressed on and began to navigate the switchbacks. Grant heard him shout out, "Stay with me!"

The urgency in his voice could only have been meant for Lillian, Grant thought. They had to make it to the Log Cabin now. McCade was too close and with Lillian wounded, they had to make the outpost soon.

CHAPTER XXII

The Log Cabin

The peaks of the Coast Mountains loomed over the small outpost that was nestled between the wild frontier borders of Alaska and British Columbia. The harsh winds howled their way through the narrow pass, cutting into every crack and crevice of the snowbound wooden structures there. The outpost at White Pass was an isolated bastion of law and order in the vast and unforgiving wilderness. Except for the whispers of treachery and danger carried on the frostbitten air, it was relatively quiet. The Log Cabin was about to face its greatest challenge yet. Tonight, it felt less like a sanctuary and more like a trap.

The door of the outpost's small but sturdy main wooden building swung open with a creak. Cold air surged into the room, making the flames of the cast iron stove's fire flicker. Constable Grant, tall and broad-shouldered, stepped inside, his face a mixture of resolve and weariness. His coat was dusted with snow, and his boots left wet footprints across the floor. Behind him, Riggs the rugged ox of a man, wore a scowl that was deeply etched onto his bearded face. An outlaw turned reluctant ally, he was the kind of man who didn't trust easily and never asked for help. But now, with Lillian badly wounded and the prospect of more danger ahead, even he had to acknowledge the need for shelter and the protection of the NWMP.

She appeared weightless in his arms as he cradled her. She was another outlaw turned ally for Grant. She was barely conscious. Her face tight with pain and her breathing was shallowed and laboured. A rudimentary blood-soaked bandage was strapped about her chest. Her collarbone had taken the brunt of the blow, a reminder of the gunfight they had barely escaped and that had nearly cost them their lives.

Unbuttoning his coat to reveal the red serge of his uniform jacket beneath, Grant's eyes fixed on the man he needed to speak to: the commanding officer of the outpost. Inspector Strickland, a man as weathered as the mountains themselves, stood by the fire, warming his hands. He looked up as Grant entered, the flicker of the stove's fires casting a sharp shadow on his prodigious moustache. His stern face betrayed the countless battles he had fought, both physical and mental, during his years on the frontiers of the great North American continent. His eyes were guarded and spoke of immediate suspicion simmering beneath the surface. When he saw the red serge jacket revealed, his expression softened.

"It looks like you brought more than just snow with you." Strickland observed, his gruff tone was more neutral than welcoming.

Grant didn't waste any time, saying "Inspector, we need to talk."

Strickland turned, his piercing gaze sweeping over the three of them. He took in Lillian's condition with a frown but said nothing, his eyes flicking between Grant and Riggs, who stood awkwardly, clearly out of place in the outpost. The sound of a crackling fire was the only thing filling the silence before Strickland spoke again.

"Your companion needs medical attention. Constable Thompson here will take your friends to Doctor Armstrong. Thompson see to it."

The young Constable was on his feet and stepped to the door. He looked up at the imposing Riggs and offered, "If you'll come with me, please?"

THE LOG CABIN

Riggs looked at the young policeman and then turned to Grant, raising an eyebrow.

"It's fine, go with them. I'll find you later." Grant told him.

"I ain't giving up my guns Copper."

Strickland replied with swift and even authority, "We're not asking you to give them up. The Doc's good, he's seen a battle or three."

With a scowl of uncertainty, Riggs turned and followed Thompson out the door.

When the door slammed shut and the cold winds abated, Strickland pointed towards his desk and the chair beside it. "Bring me up to speed. Have a seat, Constable?"

"Grant, sir. Recently of the Tagish Post." He replied as he stripped off his coat and sat in the offered chair. Grant wasted no time. "There's no time for pleasantries, Inspector. We're riding ahead of a bad situation that's headed this way."

Strickland raised an eyebrow. "Enlighten me."

"I was on patrol and taken hostage by a gang. They are organized and dangerous. It's lead by a man called McCade. They pulled off some manner of gold heist in Dawson and are headed back to Skagway."

Strickland's expression hardened, but there was no surprise in his eyes. The notorious outlaw gang had been on the run for months, a thorn in the side of the NWMP, and now it seemed they were taking desperate measures. "We're aware of the heist." He replied, "I presumed they would try to cross over here or the Chilkoot. I didn't know it was McCade though."

"They plan to attack the outpost and loot your customs duties. They plan to kill everyone and take the money."

"Damn it," Strickland muttered. "Are they far behind you?"

Grant nodded, "They're delayed, but they're coming. They want revenge for their losses."

Strickland regarded the young Constable before him in silence. He reached down to a drawer of his desk, opened it and removed a dark bottle.

"Fetch me those mugs from the stove, would you?" he directed Grant while he pulled the cork from the bottle's neck.

THE DEAD HORSE TRAIL

He watched Grant as the man stood, obviously stiff, sore and battered from the journey and walked to the stove without complaint.

"There's obviously more to this story. What losses?"

As Grant collected the mugs he replied, "We ambushed them on the west side of Turtle Mountain. Our plan was to slow them down, thin them out before they got here. The ambush didn't work, but we did cut them off from the gold. Their pack horses were separated and ran off."

"How did you manage that?" Strickland asked as Grant sat down and pushed the mugs across the desk.

"Dynamite. The woman, Lillian? She's an expert in these matters."

"Dynamite?" Strickland paused after pouring the first measure of the golden liquid. He set his jaw and then poured out the second measure. He pushed the stopper back into the bottle, set it down and gestured to Grant to take the other mug. "And the delay?" he asked.

"There was an avalanche just east of here, but they'll regroup," Grant said as he took the mug. After he drank a short sip of the whiskey, he continued, "McCade won't let something like a snow slide stop him. Now that they lost the gold, your customs duties are all they can hope to get out of this caper. That and our heads. It's become personal for him."

"The wounded pride of an outlaw," Strickland murmured as he drank from his own mug. "This avalanche, did you cause it?"

"We did what we had to do to survive."

"Also dynamite?"

Grant didn't flinch. "It was the only way to slow them down. McCade's gang is ruthless. We didn't have time for subtlety."

"Maybe," Strickland said slowly, his tone not quite convinced. "I don't like dynamite, Grant."

"I don't like it either," Grant snapped, a flash of frustration breaking through. "Sir."

"Easy, Constable. You are of course aware that you could have killed anyone in the path of these blasts. Not just outlaws?"

THE LOG CABIN

Grant held Strickland's gaze, and answered, "I was aware of the risks, sir. We had no choice. We couldn't risk McCade succeeding and killing everyone here."

"We? What's the role of your two friends in this?"

"They were with the gang. Lillian helped me to escape. Riggs, he joined us later. They both have their reasons for getting away from McCade. I wouldn't be here without either of them."

Strickland didn't respond immediately. Instead, he turned his gaze back to the fire, his mind working through the implications of everything Grant had said. This outpost had stood firm against the wilderness. Now two fugitives from the very outlaw gang that threatened its existence were at the heart of defending it.

He had seen his fair share of criminals in his time. Men and women who made deals with the devil for their survival. There was something unsettling about the duo who arrived with this unknown Constable. Strickland had learned long ago that on the frontier, loyalties were as fleeting as the snowflakes that fell from the sky.

"We can't have this place fall, Grant. White Pass a key stronghold, the entire region could fall into chaos if they overran us."

"That's why I came to you." Grant's voice was firm. "I need your men prepared. We don't have much time and it's worse than that," Grant finished off the remainder of his whiskey in a short gulp.

Strickland pushed the bottle across the desk in Grant's direction and asked, "Worse? What else do you know?"

"You've been compromised," Grant replied as he poured another tot into his mug. "Your Quartermaster Dorsey was feeding information to McCade."

Strickland stiffened, "Dorsey? How do you know this?"

"We crossed paths on the trail here. He said he was going to Bennett Lake but was dismissive when I warned him about the gang. Lillian caught him in a lie. Then he drew down on us. I shot him, wounded him and he rode off. McCade knows where and how to hit you."

The weight of Grant's words hung heavy in the room. The betrayal of a fellow constable was a bitter pill to swallow.

THE DEAD HORSE TRAIL

Strickland gave a sharp nod before acknowledging, "Dorsey, that bastard. We'll prepare for the worst." Strickland's voice hardened as he said, "I should put your travelling companions under watch. I don't trust McCade's people, current or former."

Grant felt a pang of frustration. He knew Strickland had to say it. The man was right to be wary. The betrayal of Constable Dorsey was fresh in his mind. If McCade's men had anyone else working from inside the outpost, they could tear it apart with ease.

"We don't have the luxury of time, Inspector," Grant replied firmly. "McCade's gang will be here soon. If we don't prepare, if we don't fortify, we'll be dead before the day's out. We must assume that everything you are currently doing in defence: McCade knows all about."

"We'll have pivot and to make do with what we can." Strickland said.

Turning to a nearby desk he removed a rolled up map of the region. Unfurling it, his fingers traced a line from the White Pass Outpost to the east, where the avalanche had struck. "If they're coming through the pass, they'll be forced to divert around the blockage. That'll give us some time to prepare. How many men are with McCade now?"

"I can't be sure, but I'd guess there's still a dozen, maybe more? Enough to put us on the defensive." Grant crossed his arms, his gaze sharpening. "Before I crossed Dorsey, I sent a message to Bennett for help, but we can't wait for reinforcements. The gang will hit us first. Their plan was to use sharpshooters and pick off as many of you without warning."

Strickland nodded slowly as he thought, "We'll need to fortify the outpost. Shift the Maxim position to protect it from the east. We'll move the guard positions and pull all of the scouts back to the post. We'll get things in order, Grant. You rest up. I'll need you sharp when the time comes."

Grant nodded. They had made their objective, the outpost had been warned. Regardless, he could feel the weight of the approaching conflict pressing down on him. With Dorsey's betrayal hanging over them like a shadow, the outpost was in

THE LOG CABIN

imminent danger. McCade's gang wasn't just a band of outlaws; they were ruthless, cold-blooded killers.

Strickland seemed to detect the thoughts and emotions inside Grant's mind and offered, "Doc Armstrong will take good care of your friend. Why don't you go check on them at the infirmary?" He paused, before adding, "I will need every rifle at my disposal. I'll give your friends a chance to prove their loyalty. You tell them this: if they cross me, I'll treat them worse than McCade."

Grant nodded once, a silent acknowledgment of the stakes. The look in his eyes said more than words ever could. The battle for the White Pass was about to begin. The forces of betrayal, suspicion and survival would determine who walked out of this fight alive.

CHAPTER XXIII

The Defence

The infirmary was quiet, save for the soft crackling of the fire in the woodstove and the occasional whistling of the wind outside, trying to claw its way inside. The room smelled of alcohol and herbs, the air heavy with the scent. Grant stood in the doorway, as he took in the scene before him. Lillian lay on a cot, her face pale, her breathing slow but steady. The bandages around her chest were fresh though, having been carefully replaced with clean cloth blood was already seeping through. There was no hiding the depth of the wound. She had been lucky. The bullet to her collarbone had come close to ending her life.

The lanky frame of Doctor Armstrong was leant over her as he inspected the dressings on the wound.

Grant took a slow breath, and rubbed his now clean-shaven face, trying to steady the tension in his chest. He could not help but feel the weight of the coming storm, a pressure that had nothing to do with the weather outside. *Something wicked this way comes*, he told himself. The entire outpost was about to be put to the test, and despite the preparations they had made, there was still a chance that none of it would be enough.

Beside Lillian's cot, Riggs sat in a chair, his hat tipped low over his scarred brow, arms crossed tightly over his chest. He hadn't moved much since the operation. He was too focused, too tense, too caught up in whatever thoughts were running through his mind. The two of them made an odd pair: a man who had spent his life on the wrong side of the law, and a woman who, despite her injuries, carried the weight of her past like a shackle on her wrist. In this moment, they were as much a part of the outpost as anyone, all caught up in the same storm, waiting for the same inevitable attack.

Grant stepped forward and coughed to announce his presence. He had replaced Finley's worn coat with a new heavy Buffalo coat. It rustled as he opened its buttons while approaching the cot. He didn't want to disturb Lillian, but he needed to speak to them. He needed to make sure they were ready for what was coming. He wanted to distract himself from the slow, suffocating tension of the wait before the battle. It was coming again, and no matter how much they prepared, none of them knew what the outcome would be.

"How is she?" Grant asked quietly.

The elderly Doctor's face was drawn, a weariness that only time and the compounding demands of his work could bring. He turned his attention from Lillian and did not mince his words.

"She's stable, for the time being," he said, his voice even and matter of fact. "I don't think I have to remind either of you how quickly things can change. She needs rest and time to heal. The wound was bad, but the operation went well. Still, there's a chance the fever will set in. We'll just have to wait and see."

Riggs didn't look up immediately. His fingers drummed absentmindedly on the arm of the chair, the sound sharp and steady. Finally, he spoke, his voice rough but controlled, "She's tough. She's got a better chance than most."

Grant nodded, though his expression remained grave, "Tough doesn't always cut it out here. We both know that."

"Yeah," Riggs muttered. "But it's all we've got."

"If you will excuse me. Rest is also on my agenda. I suspect things will be hotting up soon. Gentlemen," Dr. Armstrong nodded his head to both men and made his exit.

THE DEFENCE

After the infirmary door creaked shut, the silence hung for a moment longer before Riggs said, "You clean up nice. A shave and a new coat. How very respectable and civilized. What else have you been up to?"

"Helping Strickland get the men ready. McCade will be here soon enough. I don't know how much time we have."

Riggs shifted in his seat, his posture was tense, "How much of a chance do you think we really have? McCade's no fool. He'll come with everything he's got. We're outnumbered, outgunned, and this damn outpost's a sitting duck."

"That was the whole plan to start with, right? Take the sitting duck?"

"It's a well-cooked duck, that's for sure."

"Pretty fowl."

"There's no need for puns, Copper. Especially bad ones," the outlaw observed and stretched out in his chair.

"You're right, we'll be fighting an uphill battle," Grant conceded.

Riggs grunted, "If we don't make it, what happens then?"

Grant didn't immediately answer. His eyes lingered on Lillian, watching the rise and fall of her chest, the way her body was still as she fought her own unconscious battle. She had been part of McCade's gang, a criminal like Riggs, but now, with death hovering close, she was someone different to Grant. In this moment, she was just another soul struggling to survive, to hold on.

"If we don't make it?" Grant said slowly, "It's over. For all of us. The whole region could be at risk."

The outlaw didn't respond right away. He just sat, keeping his quiet thoughts unreadable. The fire crackled in the background, its warmth doing little to alleviate the chill that had settled deep in Grant's bones. They both knew what was at stake.

Riggs confirmed a morbid reality, "McCade will make sure every last one of us is dead. He doesn't leave witnesses."

"Look," Grant continued, his voice firm, "I don't know what's going to happen if we survive this but I'm not prepared to let McCade walk away the winner."

139

"I'm with you," Riggs said, and gave a stiff nod. His voice was rough, resolute, "But once this is over, what happens to us? You think Strickland's just gonna forget about the fact that we're criminals?"

Grant's gaze flickered over to the door, as if half-expecting someone to walk in. The infirmary remained silent, save for Lillian's slow, steady breathing.

"Strickland's got his own issues to deal with right now. I'm not worried about that yet."

"Yeah, well, you should be," Riggs muttered, leaning back in his chair. "Lillian and me? We're both tied up in this mess. You think anyone's going to just let us walk away after McCade's been dealt with?"

The truth was, Grant wasn't sure what would happen. "We'll cross that bridge when we get to it," he answered. "Right now, we need to make sure this place stands. We need to fight for it, or there won't be anything or anyone left to save."

Riggs exhaled sharply, pushed back his hat and ran a hand through his hair. He was silent for a moment before he spoke, "What about the fight? Where do you want me?"

Grant's eyes flickered between the two of them, "Strickland's shifted the position of his men. The Maxim gun is protected from sharpshooters, as best we can. I think you should lay in wait at the weapons magazine with the money in case they break through, then surprise them. Strickland agrees."

Riggs snorted, a dry, humourless laugh. "I can't believe he trusts us to help; after everything we've done?"

Grant thought of all the men he had served with in the Mounted Police, of the people he had met on the trails. He thought of the code they lived by honour, loyalty, duty. Their motto was 'Maintiens le Droit', uphold the right, defend the law. It often seemed like those very things would get you killed out here.

"Trust is a funny thing. You can earn it. You can betray it. Some people don't deserve it. But what happened, happened. You're here now. If we survive this, maybe you get another shot at things. Start over?"

Riggs's expression didn't change. "Survive," he echoed, his voice became almost wistful. "You think we will?"

THE DEFENCE

"There's no choice but survive," Grant said. His voice was firm, even if there was doubt lingering underneath.

Riggs nodded slowly, his hand unconsciously resting on the rifle propped beside him. His lips twitched, almost like he wanted to smile but couldn't. "Start over," he repeated quietly, almost as if tasting the words. "I've been running from something my whole life. I don't know if there's anything left to start."

Grant glanced at him, then back at Lillian, her wound still fresh and deep. "Maybe. But it's something to think about. A second chance is rare out here."

Grant stood up slowly, his gaze once again falling on Lillian's unconscious form. "We'll be ready," Grant said as he stared at her. "When the time comes, we'll fight for this place and for the people in it. After that, you have my word I'll do everything I can to get you both out here alive."

Riggs rose to his feet, the tension in his shoulders still visible, but his resolve hardening. He glanced at Lillian one last time before turning to Grant.

"Let's just hope that's enough," he said quietly. His boots scraped the wooden floor as he walked to the door, "We'd better get moving. Strickland's going to want us out there, getting ready."

Grant looked at him, then to Lillian, her face still, pale and battered. He knew what he had to do, and yet the weight of it all pressed down on him. There was so much at stake and too many lives on the line. They had only hours to fortify their defences. Every moment counted.

The cold air bit at Grant's smooth face as they stepped out of the infirmary, the door creaking shut behind them. The sharp bite of winter in the air had a way of sharpening a man's senses, making everything seem more immediate, more alive. The snow underfoot crunched beneath his boots as they crossed from the infirmary to towards the Maxim gun at the centre of the outpost. The sound of hammering and men shouting orders filled the air that coursed with tension.

Riggs fell in behind Grant, and followed closely behind, his eyes scanning their surroundings, ever watchful. The wind was tugging at the flags above the barracks. The pair of them moved

THE DEAD HORSE TRAIL

toward the small area where the Maxim machine gun had been repositioned.

As Constables were restacking its frozen sandbags and fortifications, Grant assessed its strategic position. It now was shielded from the eastern approaches towards the White Pass by the Log Cabin itself. The Mounties had also jerry-ridged a large sheet of metal to sit as a low, angled roof over the gun. It was Grant's suggestion and their best attempt to frustrate any sharpshooters from taking long shots at the men operating the gun. Their field of fire could now cover all of the outpost's other buildings if the gang broke through their lines.

Strickland was already standing by the position, his tall figure silhouetted against the backdrop of snow and ice. The man's sharp blue eyes flickered briefly toward them. His hands remained folded behind his back as he watched the horizon. He gave them a terse nod as they approached.

"We're prepared. As much as we can be. The men are ready. The Maxim can hold this position but if it fails? If they get through here, we'll be in real trouble."

Riggs stepped forward, his voice low and edged with a seriousness that only hardened criminals could possess. "I saw Dorsey's letter. It looks like you've changed most of what McCade will expect when he gets here."

"Thank heaven for small comforts," Strickland replied. "Mr. Riggs, I'd like you to help us."

"I'll guard the magazine," Riggs said without hesitation. "If they want to take the money, they'll have to go through me first."

Strickland's sharp gaze was unreadable, as he asked, "Not too much temptation for you? There's a lot of money in there."

Riggs met Strickland's gaze with an unwavering look of his own. "I've seen more. I ain't going anywhere without Lillian. You can trust me on that."

Grant exchanged a brief glance with Riggs. He had never been a man of many words, but there was something about the way the outlaw carried himself now that spoke of his commitment to their cause. He had been part of McCade's gang, yes. In this moment, there was no doubt in Grant's mind that Riggs had a loyalty far

THE DEFENCE

stronger than anyone had given him credit for. The price of survival had a way of changing men.

"Very well," Strickland said, giving Riggs a sharp nod. "Stay with the magazine. Make sure no one gets in. The rest of us will hold the perimeter."

Riggs gave a short, curt nod. "Got it."

With that, the outlaw turned and walked off, heading toward the storage building where the weapons and the precious duties were kept. His steps were measured and there was no hint of fear in his movement. Riggs was a man of action, not of words, and now he was tasked with one of the most critical jobs in the whole defence: protecting the very lifeblood of the outpost.

Grant turned back to Strickland, who was still watching the horizon, his face set in grim determination.

"I've closed the border." Strickland informed Grant. "There's a build-up of Stampeders on the American side now. We're effectively surrounded by Americans."

"Is that a concern?" Grant asked.

"Only if they choose to join in when the shooting starts." The inspector scoffed at his own joke. "We've got our positions," Strickland said quietly, his voice betraying none of the anxiety that lay beneath the surface. "I don't need to tell you how much is riding on this. I've been waiting for this moment a long time. I've been itching for a good fight."

Grant knew the gravity of Strickland's words all too well. The outpost was an expression of the country itself: the desire for peace, order and good government. The application of order and law on the frontier wilderness. If McCade's gang breached the outpost, the region would fall into chaos. People would die, resources would be lost, and the North-West Mounted Police would lose their tenuous hold over this unforgiving land.

"We're ready," Grant said firmly. "However, if we allow some areas to appear undefended, McCade will go for the easy options. We'll hit him hard if they take the bait."

Strickland nodded, though his gaze never wavered from the distant horizon. "Do you trust Riggs?"

"He's got a score to settle. He's not here to play games. He knows what's at stake. I have no reason not to trust him."

THE DEAD HORSE TRAIL

Strickland seemed to weigh his words carefully, as if debating whether to say something more. Instead, he exhaled, the breath visible in the air between them, "Just remember, if it comes down to it, we need that money secured. No matter what. We can't afford to lose it."

Grant answered, "Understood."

Another gust of wind picked up, ruffling their collars and carrying with it the faintest scent of wood smoke from the cooking fires of the Stampeders camped on the Alaskan side of the border.

The anticipation of the coming battle coursed through every fibre of Grant's being. The tension that had been building since he first arrived at the White Pass was about to reach its breaking point. They would either win or lose, and every decision made in these final hours would tip the balance one way or the other.

"You've got your orders," Strickland said, his voice low and sharp. "Get in position. I'll make sure the Maxim is ready to fire on command. We're not letting McCade take anything."

Grant gave a single, sharp nod, "You can count on me."

He turned to leave, and walked towards the barricades east of the infirmary, where his fellow Constables were preparing. He caught a glimpse of Riggs in the distance, standing at the doorway of the weapons magazine. Grant didn't know what would happen when the battle began, but he was certain that Riggs was a part of this now, just as much as anyone else.

In the end, the day's outcome would rest on the strength of the detachment and the loyalty of the ones who fought alongside them.

CHAPTER XXIV

The Attack

The cold air at White Pass hung over the outpost, heavy with apprehension. A lone sentinel against the dark wilderness, the stillness before gathering storm had grown almost unbearable for those who had never fought in a pitched battle before. Every man in the outpost knew what was coming. They had been warned, but no amount of preparation could quiet the growing sense of danger that loomed over them.

Inspector James Strickland stood near the stables at western end of the outpost, close to the American border. The flags behind him snapped and fluttered in the wind. To his left were the barracks. Directly ahead of him was the Maxim gun position, now partly sheltered from the east by the main cabin itself. Just to the cabin's left was the weapons magazine, outhouses and the store house. Just past the cabin was the small infirmary building and a series of crude barricades that his men had built next to their stacked cords of firewood.

The trail which the Stampeders and Klondikers alike had used to transit through the border crossing had packed down the snow, creating a central channel that wound its way through the outpost to the right of all the buildings. On both sides, the accumulated drifts of snow and abandoned gear had grown taller than a man. Strickland expected this route to be the conduit that brought McCade to his doorstep.

Watching the snow fall gently in the fading twilight, his clasped fingers were behind his back, tightening and relaxing their grip. His breath was slow and measured despite the quiet dread that had settled into his bones. There was no time for fear now. The gang would be here soon, and they would come looking for blood.

As he scanned the eastern approaches to the outpost he muttered to his men, "Stay sharp." It was more for his benefit than the men's.

Dorsey's betrayal had stung. If it weren't for Grant's arrival with the news about McCade, the odds would have been overwhelming. The surprise attack would have been an ignominious end to Strickland's career, if not his life. It was all but certain they would fall under attack tonight. Though, he considered, the discovery of the betrayal had also set the stage for this defence. The Mounted Police would not be caught off-guard. Every man had their orders. Now it was time to see if they were enough and could stand up to meet this threat.

His Constables were waiting at their stations, rifles ready. The weapons magazine had been reinforced, and the customs duties were locked down tight. Strickland knew they had to draw out McCade's men and hold the Pass. There were no reinforcements coming to their aid. It was the Mounties versus McCade's ruthless gang. The gang had the advantage of numbers, but the Mounted Police had their training and determination.

When the first shots rang out, they were unmistakable in their intent: you had better duck and cover. A volley of rifle shots echoed down from the northeastern side of the outpost, sharp and clean. Bullets from the chorus of gunfire snapped home and ricocheted off the steel plate above the Maxim's position.

It wasn't the opening salvo Strickland had expected, but it was enough to set the nerves of every man on edge.

"Sharpshooters," he whispered, his voice taut with recognition. "They're getting into position."

The gang had learned over the years to strike from unexpected angles. McCade knew the value of a good, long-range shot: it

THE ATTACK

keeps the defenders' heads down and made them afraid to show themselves. Now it was working on these Mounties.

"Hold fast," Strickland murmured under his breath, his mind calculating. The sharpshooters would be out on the flanks, attempting to keep their attention away from the real threat of the siege itself.

The muzzle flashes were scattered across the nearby scraggly tree line and on rocky outcrops above the outpost. Each crack of a rifle sent the defenders ducking back into cover. Strickland cursed under his breath. The gang couldn't afford to waste time with this. If McCade's men could keep them pinned long enough, they would strike at their weakest point.

"Keep your heads down," Strickland ordered, as the sound of another sharp shot cracked through the night. "They're playing with us. They want us to make the first mistake."

He then did what no man expected. The opposite of his orders, Strickland strode out from the cover of his position at the stables and walked across the main yard of the outpost.

As he walked, calm, back straight and shoulders squared, he directed the Constables at the various positions he passed. "Get to cover." he barked. Pointing at a pair of Constables behind the barracks, he instructed them, "Stay down. Wait for them to make their move."

Passing by the Maxim position, more shots pinged off the steel plate or puffed-up small sprays of snow as they struck the ground near him. "Save your ammunition, Thompson. Make your shots count."

Crouched down by the rough barricades on the easternmost side of the post, Grant was scanning the thin, nearby woods for any movement. They barricades weren't much, just hastily constructed walls of timber, snow and old crates. Looking down the barrel of his rifle, the Mountie looked worn, his face pale under the dim light of the rising moon, but his eyes were sharp and alert.

He could hear Strickland's orders being shouted out behind him. When he turned to see Strickland walking unbothered by the rifle fire around him, Grant was in awe. He had never seen such presence and calm under fire. He could hear the crunching of the snow beneath Strickland's boots as he approached, then crouched down beside him.

"McCade has something else in mind beside these sharpshooters," Strickland said, his moustached face solemn.

"I agree, something's off." Grant replied. "It's a distraction to keep our heads down."

They shared a brief, quiet understanding. A silent agreement between the two men to keep their heads and hold fast.

Strickland stood once more, and said, "Stay ready, Grant. They're coming and it'll be soon."

Grant gave a nod in reply and turned back to his position, the Winchester rifle steady in his hands.

Strickland watched the young Constable for a moment before turning to return to the outpost. When he did, a renewed flurry of rifle fire erupted with the sound of their bullet's ricochets off the timber of the infirmary's walls filling the air before the low concussive blast of an explosion shook the ground.

With a sudden, deafening boom, the storehouse to their left disintegrated into a cloud of smoke and shattered timbers.

As the scattered debris from the building began to land around them, Strickland strode off towards the smoke of the blast, drawing his revolver from its holster. His commanding voice filled the air with a strong bellow, "Stand your ground! Here they come!"

Grant looked down the barrel of his rifle and Strickland's order was proven correct. With the sound of the explosion ringing in his ears, he saw the first wave of the gang emerge from the woods a few hundred metres from his position. The outlaws didn't rush. Instead, they advanced carefully, their weapons raised.

"We're gonna have to fight for every inch," Grant muttered. He could feel his pulse quicken, but there was no room for fear now. Only action. He called out to the Constables on his left and right. "Hold them off, boys. Pick your shots. Now!"

Grant gritted his teeth as he and two other Mounties, rose up and fired off a volley of shots to keep the attackers at bay. The sharpshooters replied in an instant, firing another covering volley that sent the defending Mounties ducking back under cover.

THE ATTACK

The westerly winds caught the smoke from the explosion and blew it towards the advancing gang. As the rifle fire from the sharpshooters continued to tear through the smoke, the outlaws moved in, using the explosion as cover. As a bullet ricocheted off a nearby crate, Grant ducked instinctively, his heart pounding, but he didn't move. The sharpshooters were close now, and they were deadly accurate.

"Damn," Constable Daniels muttered from Grant's right, his eyes scanning the distant trees. "They're getting good shots in."

Grant's mind raced. He had underestimated McCade's sharpshooters. Lillian had warned him about the proficiency of their late leader, Clement. These men had learned how to use the landscape to their advantage and would pick off any Mountie who dared show himself. Grant could feel the pressure mounting with every passing second. If they didn't move, they would be overrun and killed when they hid.

"We'll need to draw their shooters out," Grant said, his voice hardening. "They want us to stay down behind the barricades. We can't let them control the pace of this fight."

Constables Wright and Daniels exchanged glances. Grant's strategy was simple, but dangerous. They needed to make the sharpshooters think they were vulnerable, then strike back fast. A brief, calculated exposure could give them the edge. If they could distract the sharpshooters, it would give them a chance to take them out.

"Are you sure?" Wright asked, his voice thick with concern.

Grant didn't hesitate, "We don't have time to be cautious. If they get inside the perimeter, it'll be over before we know it." He glanced at Daniels, his voice cold and authoritative when he said, "Daniels, you cover the right side. Wright, stay on the left. I'll give them something to focus on. You hit them, then pull back to the Maxim gun as fast as you can."

Wright nodded, his expression tense but resolute. Daniels gave a quick grunt of acknowledgment, and the three men adjusted their positions behind the barricade, weapons at the ready.

Grant watched the tree line once more, his senses heightened. Another round of gunfire rang out from the far side.

THE DEAD HORSE TRAIL

This time the muzzle flashes were much closer. He rose from his crouch and was on the move.

Keeping low and his jaw set firmly, Grant moved out from the relative protection of the barricade. A shot rang out, snapping past his head. He fired from the hip towards the tree line, forcing the sharpshooters to adjust, drawing all their attention on him.

"Dammit!" Grant snarled as he ran. He couldn't afford to be static. Another pair of bullets whizzed past him, slamming into the snow just inches from his boots.

As he sprinted trough the open space beyond the barricade, he ignored the sharp sting of the cold air slicing into his face. His boots thudded in the snow, faster and faster, but with each step, the sound of his heart seemed to grow louder, the blood roaring in his ears. He was exposed, but that was the point. The sharpshooters would be forced to focus on him.

Grant could feel their eyes on him, and he prayed that Wright and Daniels could pick off the riflemen before it was too late.

He reached the centre of the exposed area and slowed, but only for an instant. Then, he dove to the ground, flattening himself against the cold snow. A single shot rang out, tearing through the air above his head.

Grant rose again and kept moving, zigzagging in unpredictable patterns, making himself a difficult target to hit. Each time he moved, another shot echoed out, getting closer with each attempt. He knew that with each bullet aimed at him, Wright and Daniels had chances to take out the sharpshooters. They had to make this work.

From the corner of his eye, Grant saw Daniels' rifle flash as he fired, a sharp crack splitting the air. The sound of a body falling to the ground followed. One shooter down.

Wright, too, fired with deadly precision, using the cover of the barricade to his advantage. His rifle went off next, the shot echoing with a sharp, deadly report. Another of the advancing outlaws fell a gasp of wind from his last breath swallowed up by the storm.

But then, a shot rang out from a different angle. It was too close, too fast. The bullet tore through the air with a sound that was almost like a scream.

THE ATTACK

As Wright adjusted his position, Grant heard the unmistakable sound of the bullet finding its mark. The Mountie fell back from the barricade with a sickening thud, his rifle dropping to the snow beside him. Grant's stomach lurched.

"No!" he shouted and pushed himself onto his knees. He was too far away, too exposed.

Wright's body lay still in the snow. The world around Grant blurred. Panic clawed at his chest, but he couldn't afford to break his cover. Not yet.

"Wright!" Daniels screamed out from behind him. His voice was filled with rage and disbelief, but Grant couldn't take his eyes off the fallen Constable. His breath came in ragged gasps, heart hammering in his chest.

"Bastards!" Daniels growled and returned fire. His shots cut through the air, but they were wild, directed with anger not with steady aim. Another shot cracked out from shadows of the trees, in reply. Its aim was true and caught Daniels square in the throat. The Constable's hands dropped the rifle, then clutched at his destroyed throat as he sunk to his knees, falling forward into the snow.

Grant, his face a mask of fury, didn't wait. The battle was far from over. Grant's grip on his rifle tightened. There would be no mercy for those who took a Mountie down.

He rose again and took carful aim at the approaching outlaws. He fired. An outlaw fell. He racked the action of the Winchester, aimed for the next man and squeezed the trigger again. That man fell. As he racked the lever action again, he began moving to his left, smooth and methodical as he exhaled and took up precise aim on the next outlaw.

Another shot rang out from the trees, and the shot creased along the cap of Grant's left shoulder. It burned as it seared its path across the muscle.

Grant dropped prone to the snow. Breathing heavily, his heart still thudding with the adrenaline. He lowered his rifle slowly taking in the scene to his right. The bodies of Wright and Daniels were splayed out on the snow, a grim reminder of the price of holding this position.

McCade's voice called out, "Is that you Grant?" The voice was cruel. He could hear the venom in the man's taunts, "Shame about those two dead boys. That's what they get for crossing us. Just imagine what I'm gonna do to you."

Grant didn't hesitate, he jumped up, raised his rifle and squeezed the trigger, sending a shot toward the sound of McCade's voice.

McCade ducked instinctively as the bullet sliced through the air, inches from his shoulder. McCade's eyes flared with fury, and he retaliated with a shot of his own. Grant dove to the side, narrowly avoiding the bullet that crashed into the woodpile close where he had been kneeling.

"That was close Grant!" McCade roared. "You're running out of places to hide!"

From his viewpoint inside the weapons magazine, Riggs looked out through one of its embrasures. He could see the shattered ruins of the nearby storehouse, the smoke from its smouldering skeleton drifting east with the wind. He shook his head to clear the cobwebs and intense ringing in his ears. The explosion had been a stone's throw away and its concussive blast had shaken the heavy beams of the magazine and knocked him to the ground.

As his awareness cleared, he could see the gang's muzzle flashes to the east engaging the forward defences of the outpost. McCade must have had a couple of the boys sneak in with dynamite and blow the storehouse. It easily could have been the magazine they decided to hit first. They still could. With that realization Riggs scanned the scene, but the embrasure was narrow and didn't offer him a wide sightline. Strickland, revolver in hand, appeared out of the smoke.

"Riggs!" Strickland shouted out, his voice strained. "Still alive?"

"Yeah, I got one helluva headache, but I'm breathing," the outlaw replied through the gunport.

Strickland's heart pounded in his chest, looking at the ruined storehouse. He knew this was just the beginning. McCade wouldn't hesitate. Behind the burning remains of the storehouse,

THE ATTACK

Strickland saw silhouettes running away from the weapons magazine's rear wall.

"Riggs!" Strickland barked again, "Dynamite!" he screamed as he dove to one side. There was a flash of light. A thundering crash followed that sent dust and debris cascading out from the building. Another charge of dynamite.

Strickland was on his feet in a heartbeat, disoriented but not dazed. He circled the magazine and seeing the silhouettes returning from their hiding spots, he fired two quick shots into the dark. The bullets found their mark, and the shrill cry of an outlaw hit Strickland's ears.

"Riggs! Riggs!" Strickland called out as he entered the gaping hole torn out of the magazine's rear wall. "Don't shoot me!"

Stepping inside the murky light of the magazine, the explosion had thrown everything off the back wall against the opposite side of the building. He could see Riggs, was slowly moving, trying to extract himself from the pile of rubble heaped on top of him.

"Get up man," Strickland encouraged him. "I've got you covered."

Strickland's mind was honed to a single point: hold the line.

Leant against the thick logs of the back wall, Strickland took a knee and fired out the blast hole, picking off another outlaw in the dark. His movements were surgical: swift and precise but the situation was desperate.

The former outlaw groaned as he staggered to his feet, "What the hell was that?"

"You with me?" Strickland asked.

"Yeah-yeah. You got a plan?" Riggs asked in reply, his rough voice hoarse from powder smoke.

"Not a good one," Strickland replied, his eyes scanning the ground outside.

"My favourite kind," Riggs replied as he moved to another embrasure. He squinted through it, out into the darkness. His hand steady on the rifle, he aimed and fired off a single shot. It was true and he saw an outlaw collapse, another dark figure dead in the snow.

"We take the fight to them," Strickland said quickly, voice low.

"You first," Riggs replied. "What about the money?"

Strickland turned to Riggs, "It's not here. We moved it to the stables."

"You used me as bait?"

Strickland nodded grimly.

"Never trust a Copper." He grunted, "Nothing like a good double cross. Once McCade figures out the money's not here they'll go building to building to find it. You get to that Maxim gun and mow them down when they try."

"What are you going to do?" Strickland asked.

"I like your bad plan. I'm gonna take the fight to them."

CHAPTER XXV

The Last Stand

After the second explosion, Grant remained lying flat against the snow. His shoulder throbbed with pain from the rifle shot that had grazed him. Anger still swirled inside, but his resolve was clear: he couldn't let McCade win. Not now. Not after everything.

The wind carried the acrid smell of gunpowder and the echoes of the continuing gun battle from the ruined outpost.

The sound of McCade's voice was a sharp knife cutting through the night. "You're not getting away, Grant," he called out. In his growl, each word carried the weight of years of bloodshed and betrayals.

Grant eased his head up above the snow to get a view of the trees. Without warning, McCade appeared. Tall and imposing, His face was twisted into a grimace, his eyes wild with fury. His rifle raised and steady in his hands, he searched the clearing ahead for his target.

"Grant!" McCade sneered, his voice thick with malice. "I'll take you down right here. No one else, just you and me."

Grant's heart pounded in his chest. McCade was goading him, begging him to stand and be cut down by one of the sharpshooters. He wasn't ready to die here, not like this. He couldn't let McCade dictate the fight. He called out, "You'll pardon me if I don't trust your offer."

"Let's finish this," McCade said, his grin widening. "You heard me boys! Just the Constable and me in this fight."

McCade squeezed the trigger and fired. He racked the rifle's action and fired again. Both shots hissed across the clearing, none of them close to where Grant lay hidden. For a moment, his body seemed to freeze in place. The cold was nothing compared to the dread in his chest.

Another shout from McCade followed, "You think you can run forever, Constable?"

"Drop the rifle and I'll face you," Grant answered.

"You think that's going to level the playing field?" McCade replied. His lips curled into a twisted grin, his voice dripping with malice. "Have it your way. One way or another, you're a dead man walking."

McCade broke his aim and held the rifle over his head. He threw it off to one side and it disappeared into the snow. He shouted, "Rifle's gone, now show yourself boy."

Grant didn't answer, his only response a defiant tightening of his grip on his rifle. The cold air bit at his skin, but the fire in his chest was all that mattered now. The pain, the loss, it was all part of the cost. There would be no more running, no more second chances. He took a breath to steady himself and then stood, revealing himself from the snow.

Facing McCade, Grant kept his rifle raised aimed at the Outlaw's chest. The lawman's eyes burned with defiance.

The two men faced off in a silent standoff, each waiting for the other to make a move. Grant's breath was shallow as he locked eyes with McCade. There was no mistaking the hate and bitterness in the outlaw's hard, and unrelenting eyes, the kind of hate that could only be born from a man who believed he had lost everything and was ready to take it all down with him.

McCade grinned, and challenged the Mountie, "Pull that trigger and I'll see you in hell."

The world was a blur. Grant's heart pounded. Every instinct told him to retreat, to run for cover. There was no way out. His

THE LAST STAND

finger tightened on the Winchester's trigger. Snowflakes danced in the air, but his focus was locked on McCade's calculating eyes.

Grant's pulse quickened. He could end this now with one shot. The realization then dawned to Grant that this fight wasn't just about survival. It was about proving that he wouldn't go down like an outlaw. He stood for something greater that self-interest. He had to be better.

He lowered his rifle, and said, "Here I am McCade. You wanted me, now you got me."

McCade's revolver was already in hand, raised in one smooth motion, his aim steady. The crack of a shot split the air before Grant even had a chance to react. The bullet struck his left thigh with a searing pain that sent him stumbling back, the rifle slipping from his hands.

Grant kept hobbling backwards, and McCade fired another pair of shots at Grant's feet. He laughed as the Constable backtracked, then fell over the rough barricade of crates.

McCade's mocking laugh echoed across the clearing. "Pathetic," he sneered, his voice like gravel. "You're slower than I thought."

Grant's teeth gritted as he pressed down on the bleeding wound on his thigh. The world was spinning with pain. His legs felt weak, but he refused to give up. He willed himself up into a crouch against the barricade.

McCade, the predator, was slowly approaching as he mocked Grant, "Shame that was only your leg. I had hoped for a gut shot."

With practiced fingers, he plucked the three spent shells from his revolver and reloaded. As he slotting each fresh round into the cylinder the bullets gave a metallic click.

In a desperate rush of adrenaline, Grant surged around the far side of the barricade, using the cover of a broken crate to shield himself, he sprinted directly at McCade. His only hope was to close the distance before the outlaw could line up another deadly shot.

McCade's eyes widened, but he recovered quickly. The revolver's cylinder was still open. He snapped it closed with a flick of the wrist. As the gun came up again, Grant was already low, he ducked under the barrel, slamming into McCade's chest

157

with his good shoulder. Knocking the man off balance, they both tumbled to the ground, sliding across the snow in a chaotic heap. The revolver flew from McCade's hand as Grant quickly climbed on top of him, throwing a flurry of punches.

McCade roared in anger. Fighting back, his hands grabbed at Grant's shoulders, pushing him away. His fists came up, swinging wildly as they grappled, rolling in the snow. As Grant struggled to keep McCade pinned beneath him, he didn't hesitate. His fists pummelled the outlaw with every ounce of his remaining energy. His blows landed with sickening thuds, but McCade was tough, tougher than any man Grant had ever fought.

"You think you can take me down like this?" McCade hissed, his breath hot against Grant's ear.

McCade grunted with each punch Grant landed. The two men were locked in a brutal struggle, their fists slamming into each other in a storm of fury and desperation. McCade waited for an opening and then drove a sharp elbow down into the wound on Grant's leg. The Mountie saw stars from the pain and screamed as the outlaw kicked him off and escaped.

McCade rolled to his right and was standing before Grant knew what had happened. McCade's hand slid down to his side, drawing a wicked-looking bone handled knife from its sheath.

"Let's see how long you last now," McCade hissed, a twisted grin curling his lips.

As McCade swung the knife down, Grant's eyes widened as he saw the flash of steel in the pale moonlight. He barely managed to dodge the slash. The blade grazed his right cheek, sending a hot rush of blood down his face. He pushed McCade away, but the outlaw was relentless, forcing him back with another brutal swipe. When McCade's knife came at him a third time, Grant had nowhere to dodge.

The cold edge of the blade found its mark, burying itself deep into the Buffalo hide of Grant's coat and through the uniform jacket beneath it. Grant gasped as the blade scored itself across his ribcage, a searing pain radiating along the wound. McCade's grin widened as he twisted the knife back out of the coat, clearly savouring the moment.

THE LAST STAND

Grant staggered backwards, clutching at his side. He gasped in pain, the world spinning as his blood flowed freely. McCade stood over him, blood dripping from his split lip as he grinned like a madman, ready to finish what he had started.

"There's no walking away from this. Not this time," McCade sneered, pointing his knife at Grant. "You're gonna to die here, Mountie," he spat, his voice low and venomous.

Grant's vision started to fade as the pain overwhelmed his senses. His breath came in ragged gasps as the blood pooled on the snow beneath him. It felt like the end. But somewhere deep inside, a flicker of rage burned. The man was taunting him, playing with him, but Grant was done being a target. His muscles burned, his body ached, but he couldn't let up. He couldn't give McCade the satisfaction.

McCade's smug voice said, "You've been a good dog, following orders. But now you get to see the truth. You Mounties, your law, it's all a joke. I'll show you how powerless you are." He took another slow step forward, just outside of Grant's reach, the knife dangling lazily from his gloved hand.

Grant glared at the outlaw. "It's over, McCade. You've lost," his voice was hoarse, but it carried with it the certainty of a man who had been through hell and refused to give his enemy any satisfaction. He goaded McCade, "The gold's gone. You've got nothing to show for anything."

McCade's laugh was cold, low, like gravel scraping against stone. He brushed off the taunts and said, "Lost? No, no, Grant. I may have lost the gold but your scalp's gonna be my reward. I'm gonna hang it on the wall in Soapy's Parlour."

Just as McCade raised the knife for another strike, something shifted. The snap of a gunshot shattered the tension.

McCade's eyes widened in surprise as the bullet struck him low in the stomach, sending him stumbling back, his knife flying from his grasp. He howled in fury, clutching at the wound in his belly. McCade dropped, falling into the snow with a strangled gasp. As Grant's vision cleared, he could see the figure standing behind him, pistol in hand.

Lillian.

THE DEAD HORSE TRAIL

The former outlaw stepped forward. Pale as death, her expression was hard as stone. Grant saw something else gleam in her eyes: justice.

"Not today, McCade," Lillian called out. Her voice was calm, almost detached. "Not today."

McCade's face twisted with rage. He snarled, "You gut shoot me Lillian? Me?"

As his hand grasped for his revolver nearby, Lillian was not going to give him any chance. Another shot rang out, and McCade's head snapped backwards emptying its contents across the snow behind him.

Grant watched in a daze as Lillian stepped forward. When she looked away from McCade's fallen body to Grant, her expression softened ever so slightly.

"You've looked better, Grant," she said, her voice rough. "I couldn't let that bastard take you out."

Grant nodded weakly, his body shaking from the blood loss and exhaustion. The world was spinning, but for the first time in what felt like forever, there was a chance of a little peace. McCade was gone but the gang were still out there all around them.

"I appreciate that," Grant rasped. "I guess I owe you one now."

Lillian knelt beside McCade, looking down at the blood staining the snow around him. Over her shoulder she corrected Grant, "You owe me two, but who's counting?"

For a moment, neither of them spoke in this quiet aftermath, Grant allowed himself to breathe, if only for a moment. He had survived. McCade, for all his plans, had been brought to justice. A frontier justice, but it was a justice all the same. Grant had never considered that prospect valuable before, perhaps because he had never come so close to death before. The world was new and different to him now. It may have lost some of its glossy edges in the death of his naiveite, but there was a future ahead of him.

Another series of gunshots rang out, breaking the moment and drawing him back into the concerns of the present. The staccato beat of the Maxim gun joined in, and barked out a deafening reply to the rifle shots.

THE LAST STAND

After searching McCade, Lillian had transferred something to her own jacket before returning to Grant's side. She had cut away sections of McCade's shirt and removed his belt.

"This is going to hurt. We can't have you bleed out," she said and began to fashion a dressing over the wound in Grant's leg. She drew it tight with the dead man's belt.

The Constable hissed with pain as she tied it off, "Damn."

"Can you walk?"

"Let's find out," Grant replied and held out his hand.

Lillian helped him to his feet. He hopped on his good leg before testing out the other. Grant grimaced, "I'm not going to lie, that hurts like a sonofabitch but I'll live."

"Let's get you to the Doc."

"How's your wound?" Grant asked her.

"I'll be fine, I've had worse."

"I thought we were losing you. Riggs especially."

"He's just a big softy."

"Not the first description I'd use," Grant replied as he hobbled behind her.

As they passed the infirmary, the Maxim position came into view. Strickland was there, hunched over behind the young Constable Thompson who was operating the tripod mounted machine gun. As Strickland directed the gunner, Thompson pulled the trigger lever, and the steady rate of fire peppered the heavy log walls of the weapons magazine. The high-pitched metallic clatter of the weapon was continuous, as the canvas belt fed more .303 rounds into its mechanism. Its sustained rat-a-tat-tat spat fire towards the building. The gun's barrel seemed to faintly glow as the heat of its shots radiated out. The muzzle flash spat gouts of flame as its bullets struck home with a deep, guttural thuds.

Grant presumed McCade's remaining men must have been holed up there, searching for the customs duties that he and Strickland had transferred to the stables just before the attack.

After the last shots of the two hundred and fifty round belt had been fired, the Maxim fell silent but continued to churn smoke and steam from its barrel.

"Reload!" Strickland barked.

As the gun crew began to feed a fresh belt into the weapon, the Inspector called out to the remaining gang inside the magazine, "This is your last chance. Throw down your weapons and come out with your hands up and you'll live."

"Get stuffed Copper!" was the reply shouted back from inside. It was punctuated by a single rifle shot in Strickland's direction. The bullet pinged off the steel plate over the Maxim position as it struck.

As Lillian and Grant arrived at the gun emplacement's rear, Strickland turned to saw the state of Grant.

"Doctor's in the stables," he said, "You should get over there."

"When this is over," Grant replied, adding, "McCade's dead."

"Your handiwork?" Strickland asked.

"No, hers," Grant replied. "She saved me, again."

"I thank you for that ma'am," Strickland said, nodding his head to Lillian.

"Where's Riggs?" she asked Strickland.

"I'm not sure. We were in the magazine, and he said he was going to take the fight to them. I haven't seen him since."

"That's not good," Lillian observed.

"Reloaded, sir!" the gun team called out.

"Please excuse me," Strickland said to Grant and Lillian. "It's time to end this siege."

The Inspector turned away and called out to the magazine once more. His booming voice was calm and firm, and he gave the gang an ultimatum, "McCade is dead. Give yourselves up. There's nothing left to fight for. I'm giving you one minute. Make a good decision."

Inside the weapons magazine, the stark reality of the gang's situation had sunk in. The remaining six men inside exchanged heated words. Some wanted to surrender, they were cornered with no clear way to escape, and they were out of options. Others in the gang were still willing to fight, driven by hatred, defiance of the law or a misplaced sense of loyalty to their late leader.

Milton threw an empty ammo crate against the log wall, shattering it into splinters. "Nothing! There's nothing in here," he yelled. "McCade was wrong. This whole thing's gone wrong!"

THE LAST STAND

"We're done. It's time to give up," Harries pleaded to the group.

One grizzled outlaw who was crouched by the blast hole in the magazine's rear wall, growled in reply, "If we give up, we hang. Them Mounties ain't gonna let us go."

"Then we make a break for the border Riley," Milton suggested.

"Hell no. We take this to the end," countered Riley.

"I ain't dying on this mountain," Milton snapped back.

"Me neither," agreed Harries.

"Anyone tries to leave I'll shoot them in the back," Riley threatened.

"Ain't that just like you," Milton said as he levelled his revolver at Riley and fired. The bullet caught him plumb in the heart, dropping the grizzled outlaw. He was dead as he hit the floor.

"Anyone else plan on stopping me?" Milton asked, his panic filled eyes scanning the others in the room. He leant down over Riley's body and drew the dead man's gun. He pointed both revolvers at the assembled men in the magazine. "Here's what's going to happen, you all are gonna open that door and you're going to walk out and surrender to the Mounties."

"The hell we are!" Harries countered.

"Do it, or I kill every man in here." Milton's eyes may have looked crazed, but his hands and the guns in them were steady as he drew the hammers back on both revolvers.

Harries, shocked, pleaded, "Milton. Please don't..."

Looking down the barrel of a loaded and cocked pair of guns wasn't anything new to any of these men, but Milton had the drop on them and could finish off most of them before they could train their rifles on him.

"Time's up!" Strickland's commanding voice warned them from outside.

"We're coming out!" Milton shouted back. "Don't shoot us!" He indicated towards the magazine's barricaded door with one of his guns, and in a calm voice told the gang, "Get on with it. Don't keep the coppers waiting. You'll walk out there nice and slow, or you catch a bullet."

From the Maxim's gun nest, they could hear the magazine's door being unbarred. Strickland warned his gathered Constables, "Keep a sharp eye on these guys. There's no telling what they might try."

The door swung open, and the first hesitant outlaw emerged slowly. Holding his rifle ahead of him, its muzzle was upside down and pointed towards the ground. He looked back, uncertain to continue for a moment, then walked out of the door.

"Throw the weapon!" Strickland ordered the man.

The outlaw complied and in slow succession the remaining four outlaws followed suit and walked out of the magazine.

"Anyone else?" Strickland asked.

"No," came the begrudging reply.

"Hands in the air and on your knees."

Once the gang followed Strickland's instruction, he ordered the gathered Constables, "Take them."

The battle was over. The gang was broken. As the Constables shackled the hands of the survivors, they did not notice the solitary outlaw who had exited the rear of the magazine and ran for the border. The gang who surrendered were then marched at gunpoint to the stables where they were secured in one of the stalls. It would be the closest the gang would come to the customs duties they had hoped to steal.

Grant sunk down and sat on an ammunition crate next to the Maxim. He sighed with relief, "It's over."

Standing beside him, Strickland nodded with satisfaction as he surveyed the damage. The outpost had been battered, but it stood. The dead, both Mounties and outlaws, were scattered across the snow.

"We held them off," Grant said, as he wiped his face, his expression weary.

"For now. We've held the Pass, but this should be a reminder that we can never let our guard down. There will always be more like McCade out there."

It may have only been a temporary victory. The Klondike would continue to test the resolve of the North-West Mounted Police. In this moment, they had survived and in this brutal frontier's wilderness survival was victory enough.

CHAPTER XXVI

The Price

The air in the infirmary was thick with the scent of antiseptic and the faint, ever-present smell of smoke from the wood stove's fire. Outside, the wind had shifted, the bite of winter slipping its way in through the cracks in the old building. The battle had been over for nearly three days, but the cost of the assault still loomed heavy over the outpost.

Grant lay on the cot, his body sore, bruised, and covered in bandages. His side throbbed where McCade's knife had slashed across his ribs, the bullet wounds on his shoulder and thigh were bound and clean. Doctor Armstrong had just changed the dressing across his cheek and made murmurs of approval that the wounds seemed in good order. Grant's head ached but he was alive.

The door to the infirmary creaked open, and Inspector Strickland stepped inside, his silhouette framed by the dim light. He was followed by Jorge, the long rider who had carried Grant's message to Bennett Lake.

Strickland's weathered face was drawn, his usual sternness replaced by a weariness that spoke volumes of the toll the attack had taken on him.

"Grant," Strickland said dryly, but his tone lacked its usual bite. "I believe you two know each other."

Grant offered a faint, pained smile as he propped himself up on the cot. He winced from the soreness and greeted the man, "Jorge. What are you doing here?"

"I came to see how you were doing. I had to come see the truth."

"Did you find it?" Grant asked.

"I did. Your Inspector Strickland has told me everything that happened. I am sorry for the men you lost."

"Six dead," Strickland muttered, his voice quiet as he rubbed his fatigued face. "Good men. Good Mounties."

Grant's eyes fell to the floor for a moment, the names of his fallen comrades running through his head. Wright, Daniels, and the others who hadn't made it. His chest tightened, but he didn't speak. What was there to say?

Strickland continued, his voice heavier now, "Our storehouse is destroyed, supplies scattered to the wind. We're short on everything: ammunition, food, and medical supplies. The border is open again, though, which is something."

Grant nodded, feeling the weight of the situation. The Mounties had won, yes, but the cost was far too high. It had been a narrow victory, and even the aftermath would be a struggle.

Strickland leant forward, the tiredness in his eyes replaced by something harder. "Jorge is going to return to Bennett and get us some help. He'll also carry a message from me to arrest Dorsey."

Grant's head jerked up at that, "Dorsey?"

"He rode into the post after I arrived. He told them you were coming to attack them."

"The bastard, of course he did," scoffed Grant.

"I told them it wasn't right. They are holding him until I get back and let them know the truth."

"He'll be handled," Strickland said, folding his arms across his chest. "Jorge also brought news that the gold has been secured. McCade's horse-train has been picked up by the Bennett Lake Detachment. At least that's one part of the mess cleaned up."

THE PRICE

Grant grunted, his mind turning over Dorsey's betrayal. There was little time to dwell on it now. The damage had been done, and Dorsey would pay for his part in the treason.

"What do you plan on doing with Lillian?" Grant asked suddenly, the question slipping out before he could stop it. His thoughts had returned to her, to the woman who had been there at the beginning of this madness, who had stayed despite the odds. His saviour from a cruel death.

Strickland gave him a measured look and said, "She's making ready to leave. I won't stop her crossing the border. She can be an American problem."

Grant's chest tightened at the thought of her going. He held no romantic feelings for Lillian. The relationship between them had never been clear, or easy, but now the finality of its ending felt both sad and inevitable.

"I see," Grant said softly, turning his gaze to the ceiling. He wanted to say more, to ask if there was something, anything, that could keep her here. But there were no words to speak, not now.

Strickland paused, then added, "She's still an outlaw. Outlaws don't belong in our world."

Grant closed his eyes. He didn't need Strickland to tell him that. Lillian would never stay where she didn't feel she belonged, he wondered if she would ever find peace or just keep running towards the horizon.

Grant tensed, his body stiffening despite the pain, "What about Riggs?"

"Riggs," Strickland said, the word hanging heavy in the air between them. "He's dead," Strickland replied, his voice blunt, the weight of it sinking into the room like a stone dropped into still water. "We found him on the outskirts of the battle, shot full of holes. More than a dozen bullet wounds. Some of the surviving gang said he killed a score of them and kept fighting despite being riddled with bullets. He didn't go down easily."

Grant clenched his fists, his knuckles white with the intensity of his grip. Riggs, one of the old gang and yet, a man who had fought alongside the Mounties, saving lives in the end. He had proved that redemption was more than just a word. Now, he was gone. Another life snuffed out in the fires of a battle that had claimed too many.

"He deserved better," Grant muttered, his voice thick with emotion. He had seen Riggs fight with everything he had, not just for his life, but for the sake of those around him. Grant couldn't imagine what might have been next for the man had he lived. Perhaps the outlaw's death had been the best end for Riggs.

Strickland sighed heavily, shaking his head. "We all deserve better. It appears that he died as he lived, on his own terms. What more can any of us ask?"

Grant didn't respond. What could he say? The cost of the attack, the deaths, the destruction, the sacrifices made, it was more than just the men who had died. It was the toll it took on every soul who had fought and survived, the weight of it sinking into their bones, too heavy to shake.

"We'll let you rest," Strickland said. He and Jorge turned to leave, and Strickland paused at the door. "You'll be up and about soon enough. Come see me then and let's talk about what's next." He tipped the brim of his Biltmore Stetson hat to Grant as they exited.

Grant nodded without looking at him, his mind elsewhere. It wasn't long after that Grant found his feet again. Though every movement sent sharp pangs of pain through his body, he managed to dress. His clothes were blood stained, but dry. His Buffalo Coat had been darned, the bullet and knife holes mended. He steadied himself against the rough walls of the infirmary before making his way outside into the cold. Hobbling slowly with a makeshift crutch under one arm, he shuffled his way across the outpost toward the stables. The familiar scent of hay, leather, and horseflesh filled his nostrils as he walked in, his boots crunching against the frozen earth.

In the far corner of the stables, near the feed trough, Lillian stood with her back to the door. As she brushed down one of the horses, her movements were slow and deliberate. The flickering light of the lanterns inside cast dim shadows against the wooden walls. The relative quiet of the stables wrapped around them like a blanket.

Grant hesitated for a moment, and greeted her, "Lillian."

THE PRICE

At the sound of his voice, she stopped her grooming, set the brush down and turned to face him. Her usual unreadable expression unreadable and familiar distance in her eyes had been replaced. They told a calm story of decisions that had been made and roads that led in opposite directions.

"Grant," she said softly, her voice a quiet echo. "Should you be up and about?"

"Probably not," he replied, "I heard you were leaving."

"I am," she said simply, her gaze not meeting his. "After everything that's happened, I'm surprised Strickland's letting me go. I should get going before he changes his mind."

The words felt like a punch to his gut. He had known this moment was coming, but now that it was here, he couldn't escape the hollow feeling in his chest. The trust they'd shared had been fragile. Yet, they had held true to each other, relied on each other and Grant was going to miss that. There was so much he wanted to say, but it seemed pointless. Words couldn't bridge the distance between them now.

"I guess this is it," he said, his voice rougher than he intended. He looked at her, trying to make sense of everything that had happened.

"I guess so," she replied, her hands rubbing at the bridle of the horse, as if it might anchor her in the moment.

For a long while, neither of them spoke. The only sound was the soft rustle of hay and the occasional snort of a horse. The wind outside had begun to pick up again, biting through the cracks in the stables and reminding them both that the world outside was indifferent to their decisions.

"I hope you can find something out there. Something that stops you running."

Lillian shook her head, a sad smile playing at her lips. "There's that word again," she joked. "I hope so too. That would be, nice."

"Where will you go?" He asked.

"I'll cross the border," she said. "Book passage south. San Francisco maybe? You know how it is: we make do with what we've got."

"I'll never forget what you did," Grant said, emotion breaking through in his voice. He meant it though, every word. She had stood by him when things were impossible, when everyone else would've run. That kind of trust wasn't easy to come by, and it wasn't something he'd take for granted.

"Thank you," he said.

She nodded but didn't say anything, as if the weight of his words was enough. She moved to the horse's side again, gathering up the reins, preparing to saddle him for the journey ahead. She asked, "What about you?"

"I'm not sure. Back up to Tagish Post I suppose?"

"You belong here. This is your world. You and your fellow Mounties. Patrolling the wilds and restoring order."

They stood there for a long moment, neither of them speaking. Lillian reached into her coat as she approached Grant. When she opened her hand, she revealed Grant's brass pocket watch.

"You'll need to keep track of time, right?"

"Right," Grant agreed. A tear welled up in his eye as he accepted the gift and held his father's watch in his hand once more. He sniffed as he told her, "I owe you three now."

Lillian turned back towards the horse she had been tending to. her hands resting on its mane. She didn't look back at Grant as she swung up into the saddle.

"Who's counting?" she said. "Goodbye, Grant,"

Grant didn't answer. He watched he ride out of the stables, her coat fluttering when the wind caught it. As she rode away, he knew that she was leaving for good.

In the end, there were no grand declarations. There was only the understanding between them, the kind that came from shared experience—beyond words, beyond what was left unsaid. Their paths had crossed in a time of chaos, and now, in the aftermath, it was time for them to go their separate ways.

As the cold seeped into his bones, Grant let out a breath he hadn't realized he'd been holding. He stood for a while longer in the stables, holding his watch.

There was one thing he knew for sure: there would always be a place in his mind, and his heart for Lillian. No matter how far she went. He turned back toward the infirmary, there was nothing left to say: it was his silent tribute to the woman who had never been meant for his world.

CHAPTER XXVII

A New Enemy

Milton's boots squelched through the mud of Skagway's streets. He had made the trek back down the Dead Horse Trail as a Klondiker. Like many others who had ventured to the Yukon, he had been to the frontier, seen what was there, had even taken a fortune in gold; but, now returned from the wilderness penniless, with only stories to share.

His eyes darted nervously toward every shadow that loomed and shifted in the narrow alleyways of the town. He felt that everyone knew the news he carried. He feared the punishment that may be dished out on him for telling this story.

It had taken him days to get here from White Pass, days that had felt longer than a lifetime. The memory of the battle and the fortune that had been lost were still fresh in his mind. He didn't know why he was still alive and free. Maybe it was luck, or maybe it was the dark choice he made, forcing his brothers-in-arms to surrender to the Mounties to cover his cowardly escape.

There was only one thing left for him now: to bring the news back to Soapy Smith, the region's ruthless crime boss. He had been the brains behind the heist. Soapy would want to know everything: the failure, the losses, and the betrayals that had led to McCade's death. Milton didn't have much to look forward to, but at least there was the satisfaction of knowing he had survived when others hadn't. He only hoped that Soapy would show him mercy and give him some manner of paying job.

As he crossed the threshold of John Smith's Parlour, Soapy's unofficial headquarters, the warmth of the saloon's fire and the thick smell of humanity hit him. Hunger bit deep in his stomach, it had been days since he last ate. He couldn't even remember what whiskey tasted like. Cigar and pipe smoke curled about the beams of the low ceiling. The social hub of Skagway was in fine form in the dim lighting. The whiskey flowed, the gold spent, and the patrons bustled about. The plinking tunes bashed out across the keys of its battered old piano mingled with the loud cacophony of voices and clinking of glasses inside the narrow saloon's walls.

Soapy Smith was holding court, as always, his presence filling the room from the corner table he sat at. Milton pulled his coat tighter around himself, hoping to warm his bones before the inevitable confrontation. Removing his hat, he held it in both hands as a contrite supplicant. He fidgeted all the while, spinning the hat around by its brim.

As Milton approached, Soapy's cold eyes locked onto him with a mix of curiosity and suspicion. Texas Jack Vermillion, Soapy's right-hand man, sat nearby, swirling a glass of whiskey in his hand, his sharp features gleaming in the low light. He gave Milton a slight nod, acknowledging his arrival but did not appear impressed by it.

"Well?" Soapy's voice was soft but carried an edge that sent a chill through Milton. "You look like a man who's seen his share of trouble. Sit. Tell me your woes."

Milton sat down, swallowing hard as he tried to steady his nerves. He had known this moment was coming, but now that it was here, the weight of his failure pressed down on him like a thousand tons of stone.

"It's bad, Soapy," Milton began, his voice tight with exhaustion. "The Mounties at the Log Cabin, they ambushed us. We had no idea they were prepared for the attack. McCade's dead, and most of the gang's either dead or captured."

A NEW ENEMY

There was a long silence at the table as Soapy and Texas Jack processed the news. Soapy's face remained expressionless, but his fingers drummed the edge of his glass, a sign of growing frustration.

"McCade," Soapy said, his voice low, as if tasting the name for the first time. "McCade's dead, and you're telling me the Mounties stopped him?" His eyes gleamed, catlike, and his fingers stopped their drumming.

Milton nodded grimly, "Yeah. It was this Constable Grant. We caught him first and it all went wrong after that."

"And the gold? Where's my gold?" Soapy asked.

"Gone. It was this Grant again. He ambushed us and we lost all the gold."

"What about the customs duties?"

"We never got them. They moved them somewhere else."

Soapy's expression darkened. The smile evaporated from his face, replaced by a tightness around his jaw. He took a long drink from his glass, then set it down with a sharp, deliberate movement.

"A damned Constable? This Grant and a handful of Mounties bested all of you and McCade?"

"Mostly just Grant. Lillian and Riggs turned on us and joined up with him. They blew the trail and scattered our horses with the gold. We was cut off. We tried!"

Texas Jack snorted and shook his head. "One man did all of that? Some rare type of Copper right there."

Soapy's gaze remained fixed on Milton. "And you?" Soapy asked, his voice cold as death, "How did you get out of that mess?"

"I ran," Milton replied, his voice a mixture of shame and pragmatism. "When they had us all but cornered. I had to get back here and tell you what happened. The rest of the gang is gone: dead or arrested. I barely got out. The whole thing fell apart."

The room was silent for a long moment. Soapy sat back in his chair, his fingers tapping his glass as he considered the report. His mind worked quickly, calculating the next moves, assessing how this failure could be turned to his advantage.

THE DEAD HORSE TRAIL

"Let me get this straight," Soapy said. "This Constable Grant turned two of McCade's best people, tricked McCade, blew up my gold, killed McCade and otherwise killed or captured the rest of the gang. There's no money and all I have to show for it is you?"

Milton nodded, "That's what happened."

For a moment, Soapy just stared at Milton, his eyes calculating the man before him. Finally, he set his glass down with a sharp click on the table.

"Where's this Grant now?"

"Up the mountain, White Pass I'm guessing."

"What about Lillian and Riggs?"

"I dunno about Lillian. Riggs is dead."

"You're sure?"

"Yeah, he took about a dozen bullets, but he went down in the end."

"He was a monster of a man," Texas Jack offered.

"He was a traitor!" Soapy snapped back, before pointing a long, well-manicured finger at Milton. "I don't take kindly to being double crossed!" His voice was seething with anger, "McCade could be unhinged, but I never thought him a fool. This Mountie thinks he's won?"

For a long moment, Soapy just stared at Milton, his mind working. Texas Jack remained silent, his cold eyes flicking between the two men.

Soapy stood, his tall frame casting a shadow over the table, "This isn't over." He walked to a small window, his back to Milton. "I didn't ask for excuses," he said, his voice ice cold now. "I asked for results. When there's gold involved, I require a result."

Milton flinched at the word. Soapy's anger was the stuff of legend, and he feared what came next. He'd seen this side of Soapy before. When things didn't go as planned punishment was dished out. Swift, violent and decisive punishment.

Soapy turned slowly, and Milton felt his knees shake as the man's remorseless eyes held his own. He instinctively shifted back in his chair, his voice faltered as he stammered, "I did what I could."

"What you could?" Soapy repeated. "I gave McCade a chance," Soapy continued, his voice dangerously calm. "I trusted

174

him to handle this. Instead, he's dead. Let me tell you something, Milton. When you disappoint me, it's not about failure. It's about weakness. You think I don't see it? You think I don't know exactly who I'm dealing with? Do you know what that means?"

Milton opened his mouth to answer, but Soapy silenced him with a raised hand.

"It means that you are useless to me. I should kill you right here, right now. But that wouldn't help. It wouldn't make things right," he paused, as if letting the words sink in, "It would make me feel better though."

Milton's throat went dry. He knew he wasn't out of the woods yet. "I'll make it up to you, Soapy," he said quickly, almost pleading. "I'll make it right. I will. Just give me a chance."

Soapy leaned in close, his voice dropping to a whisper, the air around them growing thick. "You've already had your chance and I'm done being patient with you."

Milton's heart hammered in his chest. "Please. I'll do whatever you need. Just don't let this be the end for me."

Soapy straightened up, his gaze never leaving Milton's face. He tilted his head, considering Milton's words and threw a look at Texas Jack. Still reclined in his chair, he rested a hand on the grip of his revolver and asked, "What's the plan, Soap?"

Inside the outline of his pointed Mephisto beard, Soapy's lips curled into a slow smile. It was one that promised trouble.

"Milton wants to make it right."

Texas Jack stood up, a predatory grin spreading across his face. Milton's heart skipped a beat. He instinctively raised his hands in surrender.

Soapy's gaze locked with Milton's, and asked, "How are you going to make this right? This Grant has ruined everything. He's the reason McCade's dead. He's the reason you're standing here instead of enjoying your cut of what was rightfully ours."

Milton's stomach twisted, but he knew there was no choice. He had one way out. "I'll do it," he said, his voice shaky but determined. "I'll take care of Grant."

Soapy's smile widened, but it wasn't a kind smile. It was the smile of a man who had just ensured his hold over Milton.

"What are you saying?"

"I'll do it. I'll kill Grant for you."

"Good," Soapy said softly. "You better. This is your last chance. If you don't, I'll make sure you regret it. Your life won't just be over, you'll wish I had killed you here today."

Milton nodded, the weight of the task pressing down on him, "I won't let you down."

Soapy gave a sharp nod, "See that you don't."

After Milton had left Texas Jack and Soapy stood by the bar. As his boss lit a fresh cigarillo, Texas Jack watched Soapy with a sharp gaze, waiting for his next move and asked, "Think he'll do it?"

Soapy didn't answer right away. He was staring at the door where Milton had just disappeared, his fingers rhythmically tapping the edge of his glass. His face was hard, his mind calculating, weighing the consequences of this latest development. His voice was dangerous as he replied, "Doesn't matter. One way or the other we'll never see Milton's face again."

He drained the contents of his glass with a sharp flick of the wrist and then poured out another measure from the bottle beside them.

"Of course, I could be wrong. I do trust that Milton is a rat. When you threaten a rat and back it into a corner, it'll fight to survive. He'll go to White Pass and do what I need. Or, he'll die trying."

Jack chuckled darkly as they stepped away from the bar and returned to their table with the fresh bottle.

"Either way, he'll deal with Grant or Grant will know that he's a marked man."

"Yeah?" Jack's grin widened. "Ain't no second chances with you, Soap. This Mountie's gonna be trouble, I can feel it like a sliver in my palm."

Soapy's eyes flicked towards Jack, a spark of irritation flashing in his gaze before he calmed himself. "If Milton can't do it, then you and I will make sure Grant doesn't make it out of the Klondike alive." His voice was almost a growl, "Put a bounty on his head. Big enough to make every lowlife and outlaw think about it. They'll come for him, and they'll do the job for us."

Jack's eyebrows lifted in surprise, "A bounty on Grant?"

"Not just any bounty," Soapy said, leaning closer to Jack, his eyes glinting. "The kind of bounty that will turn every man with a rifle or a pistol into an eager volunteer. He'll have every scavenger, every bandit and desperate fool on his tail. If he survives the first week, I'll be impressed."

Jack chuckled darkly, his hand hovering over his glass, but he didn't take another drink. "It's a risky move. The Mounties won't take kindly to it."

"The Mounties can do whatever they want. They're over there and I'm right here."

Jack's grin was slow but deadly. "What if someone gets to Grant first, someone other than you?"

Soapy's smile stretched into something dark and predatory. "It doesn't matter so long as he's gone. If some other fool takes the credit for it, that's fine by me. Cheaper too."

Jack gave a short, bitter laugh. "You're always thinking two steps ahead. I'll get the word out. We'll make sure that bounty gets around."

"Make sure it's good and loud," Soapy said, his voice dropping lower, darker. "The bigger the prize, the more eager they'll be. I want Grant's name on every damn tongue between here and the border."

"How much are we talking?" Jack asked, his hands moving as he reached for the bottle.

"I want it high enough that every man worth a damn will be willing to risk his life for it. A thousand dollars. No, make it two." Soap replied and laughed.

Jack's eyes widened. "Two thousand? You're serious?"

"Dead serious," Soapy said, his voice steeled with resolve.

Jack nodded, emptied his glass and stood up, backing his chair away from the table. "I'll see to it. You want it posted in Skagway first?"

"Skagway, Juneau, Dawson, the whole territory. I want every man with a gun to know who to target; and who's paying the bill."

"Grant's made a mistake. He's crossed me, and there's no turning back. Let them come for him, Jack. Let them tear him apart. I'll be waiting for the day when his body is found, a bullet in his skull, and the name Soapy Smith on everyone's lips."

Jack lingered for a moment, his hand on the door handle. "You're a dangerous man, Soapy. But I've learned that's why we're all still standing."

CHAPTER XXVIII

A New Post

Standing near the wood stove of the Log Cabin, Grant felt the radiating heat of the stove warming the back of his legs. The past weeks of rest and recovery had been long, and while his body had been healing, his mind had been slower to catch up. The wounds inside remained deep and unseen. They had changed him. The gunshots, the betrayals, McCade's cold face, and Riggs' last stand, each had left a mark that no amount of rest could heal. The scar McCade's knife had cut across his cheek had knit well and now gave his appearance a new edge of menace.

White Pass, with its crisp, icy winds and the ever-present shadow of the mountains felt more like a cage than a refuge. The outpost had been secured, but its survival had come at a price. Good men had died. Buildings had taken damage. Supplies had been in short supply until Jorge and the Bennett Lake Mounties arrived to replenish them. The Mounties who remained at White Pass were tired, their morale dented, but they had kept to their duty and felt a grim pride in holding their ground.

"We must talk today," Strickland had said to him earlier that morning. The words haunted Grant as he waited in the cabin for Strickland's arrival.

"Feeling better, Constable?" Strickland's greeted him as he entered the cabin. As he stomped the snow from his boots, the Inspector's face was hard, and the weariness that had been there before was gone. He looked like a man who had faced immense odds and knew that the weight of his duty could not be shrugged off. He would rise the next challenge and the one after that.

"Getting there, sir," Grant replied.

Strickland motioned for him to sit, and Grant did with no small sense of relief. The wounds were healing, but they still ached with a vengeance. His eyes lingering for a moment on the map of the region pinned to the wall, the lines marking the outpost's tenuous grasp on this land. Beyond it lay the wilderness of the Klondike and the lawlessness that continued to persist despite their efforts.

"Are you fit to travel?" Strickland asked, his voice softer now.

Grant glanced at the map again and nodded his head. "I am, sir. I should be getting back to my post."

"The thing is Grant, there's no need for you to return." Strickland said and leant forward, his hands clasped. "I'm seconding you to my command. I need to make best use of all the resources available to me.

"Sir?"

"This post, this little slice of civilization, is the only thing standing between the law and frontier chaos. White Pass is a chokehold for the entire region. Without it, the border would be wide open. The law would be nothing more than a suggestion. You've seen it for yourself."

"I've seen enough to know it's not that simple," Grant muttered. "The law, it's not as clear-cut for me anymore. It's not clean. And it sure as hell isn't always right."

Strickland allowed a moment to pass between them. He agreed, "No, it's not. We don't have the luxury of second-guessing every decision. We enforce the law the best way we can, no matter how dirty or difficult it gets. That's the reality of this place."

Grant thought of the faces of the men who had died. He thought of Riggs, who had kept fighting to the bitter end alone, wounded and outnumbered. He thought of Lillian, her departure

A NEW POST

still lingering like a shadow. She had been able to walk away, seeking something that had eluded her here, and Grant couldn't blame her.

Strickland leaned back, his eyes scanning Grant's face as if measuring his resolve. He said, "I'm asking you to stay, Grant. I need someone to handle a special assignment. It will not be clear cut. It will be dangerous, and I need someone who can handle themselves, think for themselves and solve problems."

"What's the assignment?"

"First, we need to get these customs duties out of here and safely shipped back to Ottawa. You'll take a small detachment and escort the funds to a ship in Skagway. I don't have to tell you that there's a lot of criminal interest in this money. You'll likely come up against the man behind the McCade's gang: Soapy Smith."

"I've heard of him," Grant replied, unfazed. "What's the other part?"

"I need you to manage the post. The mail that's come in at Skagway has piled up. Tens of thousands of letters I'm told."

Grant looked up sharply, surprised by the request. "You want me to deliver the mail?"

"Not just mail," Strickland said, his gaze sharpening. "I want you to secure our link to the outside world. It's a delicate situation. Skagway was a hive of villainy and predators long before McCade's attack. We can't afford to let the law slip. We can't afford to compromise our position and authority."

Grant felt the weight of it settle on him, the enormity of the task hanging like a dark cloud. He had always believed in the law, in what it stood for. But now, after all he had seen, could he still believe in it the same way? Was he capable of pushing forward, knowing the compromises and darkness that came with it?

"The post must get through," Strickland said, as if reading his thoughts. "No matter what it takes. This isn't just about law and order. It's about the stability of this region. If we fall, everything falls with us. Regular, reliable mail service is a part of law and order. We have been tasked to fix that problem. You unders' that don't you?"

THE DEAD HORSE TRAIL

Grant nodded slowly, the gravity of the words settling in his chest. He could feel the shift within himself. The man who had first walked into White Pass, eager and idealistic, was gone. He had faced too many hard truths, seen too much blood spilled. The law was no longer a perfect ideal for him. It was something to uphold, but when there was no other choice: survival now trumped the law. It was the only way through this wilderness, this life of unexpected violence and uncertainty.

"I'll stay," Grant said quietly, his voice steady despite the turmoil inside. "I'll handle Skagway's post. I'll make sure everything gets through."

Strickland looked at him for a long moment, then gave a slow nod, as if he had known what Grant's answer would be all along. "Good. You're a man of your word, Grant."

Strickland turned toward the door, his posture relaxed but his expression still hard. "I'll have your orders drawn up. You get yourself together and pick three Constables to go with you. There's a lot of work ahead."

Grant nodded, rose and saluted Strickland. After stepping out of the cabin, he stood on its porch for a long moment, letting the silence of the mountain air fill him up. Staring out at the western horizon, the cold expanse of snow and mountains stretched away from him towards the North Pacific and Skagway.

The world was unforgiving. The law was complicated. Grant knew he had to push forward, even when the lines between right and wrong blurred into nothing more than shadows. There was a new challenge ahead of him. A new future and duty was calling out and it lay across the mountains in America.

As Strickland had said, "The post must get through." It was all that mattered now.

Manufactured by Amazon.ca
Bolton, ON